청어詩人選 329

안봉자의 제4 한영대역시집

Bong Ja Ahn's Korean-English Poetry Anthology IV

Songs from the Lotusland

로터스랜드에서 부르는 노래

Translated by the Author

저자 역

청어

Songs from the Lotusland / 로터스랜드에서 부르는 노래
Copyright ⓒ 2022 by Bong Ja Ahn

Author: Bong Ja Ahn
Publisher: Chung-eo Publishing Company

Songs from the Lotusland / 로터스랜드에서 부르는 노래
안봉자 지음

발 행 처 · 도서출판 청어
발 행 인 · 이영철
영　　업 · 이동호
홍　　보 · 천성래
기　　획 · 남기환
편　　집 · 방세화
디 자 인 · 이수빈 ｜ 김영은
제작이사 · 공병한
인　　쇄 · 두리터

등　　록 · 1999년 5월 3일
(제321-3210000251001999000063호)

1판 1쇄 발행 · 2022년 5월 10일

주소 · 서울특별시 서초구 남부순환로 364길 8-15 동일빌딩 2층
대표전화 · 02-586-0477
팩시밀리 · 0303-0942-0478

홈페이지 · www.chungeobook.com
E-mail · ppi20@hanmail.net
ISBN · 979-11-6855-034-6(03810)

Songs from the Lotusland

로터스랜드에서 부르는 노래

안봉자의 제4 한영대역시집

Bong Ja Ahn's Korean-English Poetry Anthology - Ⅳ

I dedicate this book to my husband,

Jin W. Lee

마추픽추에서

Lotusland:

A nicknamed for Vancouver, B.C., a port city on the west coast of Canada.

The nickname was given to Vancouver because of its mild climate, beautiful nature with good infrastructure and excellent urban design harmonizes peacefully. The word 'Lotusland' is derived from Odyssey IX's 'Lotus-eaters' by the Greece ancient poet Homer.

로터스랜드:

캐나다 서해안 브리티시 컬럼비아주 항구 도시인 밴쿠버의 애칭.
온화하고 아름다운 자연과 좋은 사회적 구조 및 세련된 디자인의 도시 밴쿠버에 붙여진 별명이며, '로터스랜드(Lotusland)'라는 말은 그리스의 고대 시인 호메로스의 「오디세이 9권」에 나오는 'Lotus-eaters(연꽃 먹는 사람들)'에서 파생되었다.

✤ 감사의 말씀

시(詩)에 대한 나의 열정을 이해하고 항상 정신적으로 성원해주는 남편과 장성한 세 아들, 그리고 그들의 사랑스런 가족에게 늘 마음으로 감사하고 있습니다. 이들의 이해와 정신적 성원이 없다면 오늘의 "시인 안봉자"는 없었을지도 모릅니다.

이 책의 원고를 꼼꼼하게 읽어주시고 귀중한 조언을 해주신 미국 벨링햄의 시인, 교육자이며 교정사이신 Betty Scott 님께 진심 어린 감사의 마음을 전하고 싶습니다.

나의 영문시 창작 초기 시절부터 시에 대한 나의 재능과 열정을 알아보고, 캐나다에서 이중 언어 시인의 꿈을 키우고 있는 나에게 여러 가지로 도움의 손길 뻗어준 Ariadne Sawyer 여사와 Ashok Bhargava 님에게 특별한 감사를 드립니다. 나에게 그들과의 인연은 큰 행운이며, 그들과의 아름다운 우정을 나는 영원히 간직할 것입니다.

이제까지 쓴 나의 아홉 권 저서 중에서 가장 큰 의미를 지니는 이 시집 "Song from the Lotusland / 로터스랜드에서 부르는 노래"를 출판해 주시는 고국의 청어출판사 이영철 대표님과 방세화 편집장님께, 그리고 지금 어디에선가 이 책을 읽고 있는 나의 독자님들께, 감사와 사랑을 드립니다.

여러분, 진심으로 감사합니다.

안봉자

✤ A Note of Thanks

I am very grateful to my husband and three grown-up sons and their loving families, for understanding my passion in poetry and giving me mental support all these years. Without their mental support, I don't think I could have made this far.

I would like to express my heartfelt gratitude to Ms. Betty Scott the wonderful poet, educator, and editor in Bellingham, USA, for editing the original manuscript of this book and providing invaluable suggestions.

My special thanks go to Ms. Ariadne Sawyer and Mr. Ashok Bhargava for their belief in my poetry from the very early days of my English poetry writing, and have been helping me to become a bilingual poet in Canada. I feel very fortunate to meet them, and I will cherish the beautiful friendships with them forever.

I like to extend hearty thanks to Mr. Young-Chul Lee the president of the Chung-eo Publishing Company in Seoul, Korea, for publishing this book "Song from the Lotusland / 로터스랜드 에서 부르는 노래" which is the most purposeful piece of work among the nine books I have written so far, and to my readers reading this book somewhere, now.

Thank you all from the bottom of my heart!

Bong Ja Ahn

✚ Foreword

Ashok K. Bhargava

『Songs from the Lotusland』 is an anthology of Bong−Ja Ahn's new and selected poems, penned in various contemplative moods. These poems like a kaleidoscope, reflect on changing thoughts, feelings, emotions and perspectives. It sheds well−tempered light on the variety and scope of Bong Ja Ahn's artistic merits as a poet.

This book celebrates half a century of loving togetherness of a wedded life of Bong−Ja Ahn and her husband, as well as fifty years of life as immigrant and naturalized Canadians. I met Bong−Ja in 2003 and invited her to read poetry at the Strawberry Hill branch of Surrey Public Library. Over the years I discovered that her life has beauty of a fragrant spring flower, a shining vibrancy of autumn leaves and sweetness of glossy red fruits that attract winter songbirds.

These poems take you on an exciting journey through moving from one continent to another, frustrations which arise from re−rooting in a different soil, love and compassion. In 'Dancing Auroras' and 'Christ the Redeemer' she provides an intelligent and acute understanding of different continents, surroundings and cultures.

As a new immigrant to Canada, in 'One Rainy−day Afternoon' she forges ahead with a resolute resilience, wanting to build rainbow dreams again with young family. Her poems about experiences in an alien culture are inspiring and optimistic.

The rendering of personal experience in 'Fried-Egg-Flower' is modest, stark, yet powerful. In fact, the strength of her verse lies in its very simplicity. In 'I Am Sorry', she is adept and forceful in her expression in the acquired language as she is in her native one.

There is a grandeur in the simplicity of her verses and a wealth of meaning in her short, succinct and sublime poetry. By the time one finishes reading her poems, one is suffused with a robust energy of hope, and of love.

This bilingual poetry anthology 『Songs from the Lotusland/로터스랜드에서 부르는 노래』 is highly recommended for everyone, especially for those amongst us, who appreciate tenderness of soft compassion.

Ashok K. Bhargava:
An award-winning multilingual poet; The founder and president of the Writers International Network Canada(WIN Canada); Community activist; public speaker; Former president of Literary Society of BC; Author of six poetry books and many poetry anthologies.

✢ 서문

애쇼크 바가바

『로터스랜드에서 부르는 노래』는 안봉자 시인의 신작 시들과 전에 출간된 책들에 발표된 시들 중에서 엄선한 시(詩) 모음집이며, 다양한 각도로 모든 사물이나 형상을 차분히 들여다보는 관조적 분위기를 담았다. 이 책에 담긴 시(詩)들은 만화경처럼 수시로 변화하는 안 시인의 생각, 느낌, 감정 및 관점을 그때마다 반영하며, 자신이 지닌 시인으로서의 예술적 다양성과 광범위함의 장점을 훈훈하게 발산한다.

이 책은 안봉자 시인이 남편과의 결혼생활 반세기와 캐나다에 이민 와서 캐나다 사람으로 동화되어 살아온 지난 50년을 아울러 기념하기 위하여 엮어낸 것이다. 내가 안 시인을 처음 만난 것은 2003년이었다. 그때 나는 그녀를 써리 시(市) 공립 도서관 '스트로베리 힐'로 초청하여 시 낭송을 하도록 했다. 그 후 20년 가까이 함께 문학 활동을 해오면서 나는 그녀의 삶 속에 담긴 향기로운 봄꽃의 아름다움과 가을 단풍잎의 타는 정열과 겨울 울새(song bird)들을 유혹하는 윤기 흐르는 붉은 과일의 달콤함을 발견했다.

이 책의 시(詩)들은 한 대륙에서 또 다른 대륙으로 이동하며 펼쳐지는 안 시인의 흥미진진한 여정과 그녀가 이민의 땅에 새 뿌리 내리며 느껴야 했던 당혹감 및 사랑과 연민의 세계로 독자들을 안내한다. 시「춤추는 오로라」와「구원의 예수상 앞에서」에서 안 시인은 그녀가 직접 보고 느낀 여러 대륙의 다른 환경 및 문화에 대하여 정확한 지식과 이해를 우리에게 제공해준다.

캐나다 이민 초창기 시절의 한 이야기를 다룬「어느 비 내리는 오후」에서는 한 젊은 가족이 이민의 땅에서 '밝은 미래의 무지개 꿈'을 반드시 이루겠다는 개척자의 단호한 결단력과 미래를 향해 나아가는 비장한 모습을 보여준다. 그렇게 타문화 속에 정착하는 삶의 과정에서 체험으로 탄생한 그녀의 시들은 다분히 고무적이고 낙관적이다.

안 시인 자신의 어릴 적 기억을 묘사한 시 「달걀부침 꽃」은 소박하고 꾸밈없으면서도 강한 힘을 가졌다. 사실, 안 시인 시들의 힘은 바로 그 지극히 단순함에 있다. 또 다른 시 「미안해요」에서 그녀는 모국어처럼 숙달된 언어로 능숙하고 능란하게 감정을 표현한다.

그녀의 시어들은 단순함 속에 웅장함이 있고, 짧고 간결하며 정화된 시어들 속에 풍부한 의미가 깃들어 있다. 그래서 누구든 그녀의 시들을 다 읽고 날 때쯤이면 어느새 희망과 사랑의 강한 에너지가 가슴에 가득히 차오르는 것을 느끼게 될 것이다.

이 이중 언어 시 모음집 『Songs from the Lotusland / 로터스랜드에서 부르는 노래』를 많은 사람, 그중에서도 특히 부드럽고 차분한 감정 이입의 시(詩)를 좋아하는 이들에게 적극 권한다.

애쇼크 바가바:
여러 문학상 수상 경력의 다국어 시인, 국제 작가 네트워크 캐나다 협회(WIN, Canada) 창립자이며 초대 회장, 지역 사회 활동가, 대중 연사, 브리티시 컬럼비아주 문학부 협회 회장 역임, 6권의 시집과 많은 시선집의 저자.

50년 세월의 화폭에

참으로 긴 공백기였다. 지난 몇 년간 나를 괴롭혀오는 극심한
안구건조증에 나는 정신적으로나 육체적으로 지쳐 있었다.
그렇게 무기력 상태에 빠진 나에게 죽비를 내려준 것은
아이러니하게도 코로나바이러스였다.
작년(2020년) 3월, 코비드-19 전염병이 온 세계를 강타하고
사람들은 '사회적 거리 두기' 혹은 '집콕'이라는 불편한 현실적
상황에 싫든 좋든 길들이며 살아야 했을 때, 나는 그동안 미뤄오던
나의 아홉 번째 저서를 이참에 끝내기로 작정했다.
그리고 새 책 편집에 혼신으로 매달렸다.
그러다가 안타깝게도 대상포진이라는 질병에 걸렸고,
뒤늦게 고약한 오미크론에 감염되어 투병하다보니 나의 작업은
또다시 마냥 지연되고야 말았다.

오늘, 나는 드디어 나와 내 남편의 결혼 50주년과 우리의
캐나다 이민 50주년을 아울러 기념하는 나의 아홉 권째 저서이자
네 권째 한영대역시집『로터스랜드에서 부르는 노래 /
Songs from the Lotusland』의 편집을 모두 끝마쳤다.
세월의 빠름이라니!
1970년 12월, 그때 붉은 뺨의 20대 중반의 내가
노스웨스트 비행기의 트랩을 내려오며 가슴 설레며 훑어보던
눈 덮인 밴쿠버의 그림처럼 아름다운 산천 위로

그 후 반세기라는 세월이 흐른 것이다.

처음 30여 년 이민의 삶은 땀으로 범벅된 도전의 연속이었다.

그 와중에 시(詩)를 쓴다는 것은 생각하는 것조차 사치였다.

내가 조기 은퇴 후, 캐나다 현지 영어권 시인들과 어울리며

한/영 이중언어로 시를 써온 지 20년이 되었다.

언어와 문화적 배경이 전혀 다른 이민지에서 영문으로

시를 창작하는 일은 또 한 번 부딪혀야 할 큰 도전이었다.

『로터스랜드에서 부르는 노래 / Songs from

the Lotusland』에는 그동안 내가 쓰고 번역한 300여 편의

영/한시 중에서 내가 직접 선별한 60편의 시들이 수록되었다.

60편 중 15편은 전에 이미 출판된 나의 세 권 영한대역시집에서

선택한 것들로 나의 이민 초창기 때의 모습이 담긴 회고록 시들을

포함한, 나에게 이런저런 이유로 특별한 의미를 부여하는

시들이고, 나머지 45편은 나의 제3 영한대역시집

『By the Fraser River / 프레이저 강가에』(2016) 출간 이후에

써서 여러 신문과 문예지에 발표한 신작 시들이다.

어떤 시들은 영어로 먼저 감각이 와서 영어로 쓴 뒤 나중에

한국어로 번역했고, 또 어떤 시들은 한국어로 먼저 쓴 뒤

나중에 영어로 번역했다. 그들이 어떤 언어로 먼저

시작되었냐에 관계없이, 이중 언어와 이중 문화권 속에서

살아온 나의 시들은 두 언어로 한목소리를 내고 있다.

이 책 『로터스랜드에서 부르는 노래 / Songs from

the Lotusland』는 아마도 지금까지 쓴 나의 아홉 권 저서들

중에서 내게 감정적으로 가장 뜻깊은 책이라 할 수 있겠다.

1967년에 제정된 캐나다 신이민법, '점수제'의 첫 물결을 탄

캐나다 한인 이민 1세대의 하나인 나와 남편이
산 설고 물 선 이민의 나라 캐나다 밴쿠버에 정착하여
지난 50년간 땀 흘려 이루고 보듬어 온 삶의 순간들을 내 영혼의
붓으로 세월의 화폭에 그려낸 인생 삽화 모음집이기 때문이다.
70년대 초에 온 대부분 한인 이민자들이 그러했듯,
우리의 유일한 자산인 '청춘'을 송두리째 저당 잡히고
이민이라는 척박한 영토에 제2의 인생을 접목한
우리 부부의 소중한 삶의 이야기들–
비가 오나 해가 나나, 기쁘나 슬프나 한결같이
반백 년을 손에 손잡고–
때로는 잃는 중에 얻으며,
때로는 얻는 중에 잃으며,
그러나 결코 삶에의 믿음을 잃지 않으며….

2021년 10월
리치먼드 바닷가 '스티브스톤 빌리지'에서
안봉자

50 Years on Canvas of Time

It was indeed a long slackness. The severe Dry Eye
Syndrome for the past few years has made me exhausted
mentally and physically. Ironically, it was Coronavirus that
gave a wake−up push while I was dawdling in helplessness.
In March 2020, when Covid−19 hit the world hard, and
people, whether like it or not, had to live with
the uncomfortable reality of 'Social distance', 'Stay home',
I decided to take advantage of the situation, and finish
my ninth book which I had been procrastinating on.
I fully immersed into editing the new book. But
unfortunately, I fell ill with Shingles, followed by nasty
Omicron, and my work got delayed again.

Today, finally, I completed editing my 9th book and 4th
volume of English/Korean poetry 『로터스랜드에서 부르는
노래 / Songs from the Lotusland』 to commemorate
my and my husband's 50th wedding anniversary,
as well as the 50th year of our immigration to Canada.
How time flies!
Half a century has flown since that day, December 1970, I in
my mid−twenties, looked over the picturesque snow scenery of

Vancouver with throbbing heart from the stairs
of Northwest Airlines.
The first 30 years of my "Immigrant Life" was sweaty and full
of challenges; Writing poetry was a luxury even thinking of it.
It has been twenty years since I retired early and began
writing poetry in English with local English-speaking poets.
With a diffrent mother tongue and cultural background,
writing poetry in English has been a big challenge.

This book contains 60 poems which I carefully selected
from 300 bilingual poems that I have written over the years.
15 of the 60 poems are chosen from my three previously
published bilingual poetry books because, for one reason or
another, they hold special meanings to me, including poems
from the memoirs of my early days of immigration.
The other 45 are from newer ones, have written and
published in the newspapers and literary magazines
since my last publication:
『By the Fraser River / 프레이저강가에』(2016).
Some of my poems began as expressions in English and
translated into Korean, while others started in Korean and
translated into English later. Regardless of how they began,
I, both bilingual and bicultural, translated them so that every
poem speaks one voice in two languages.

This book 『Songs from the Lotusland / 로터스랜드에서
부르는 노래』 is, perhaps, the most emotionally purposeful

piece of work among my nine books I have written so far.
Because this is a collection of life illustrations drawn with
the brush of my soul on the canvas of Time; The life of me
and my husband's sweaty moments as one of the 1st generations
of Korean−Canadian who rode the wave of
'Immigration Act of Canada 'Point System' 1967',
settled and built a new life in Vancouver for 50 years.
Like most Korean immigrants in the early 1970s,
we mortgaged our only asset 'youth', and tried very hard
to graft our second life in the barren land of Immigration.
Rain or shine, highs and lows, hand−in−hand all along
for the half century.
Sometimes, gained while losing.
Sometimes, lost while gaining,
yet, never lost faith in life.

October, 2021
From 'Steveston Village' by the sea
Bong Ja Ahn

✛ 차례 CONTENTS

Part One　GONE ARE THE DAYS
제1부　그때 그 시절

Part Two   THE COLOURS OF A LIFE
제2부   삶의 색깔들

Part Three   MY ISLAND
제3부   나의 섬

Part Four　ON THE ROAD AGAIN
제4부　다시 길 위에서

Part Five   FRAGRANCE OF HUMAN−FLOWER
제5부   인간 꽃 향기

Part One
제1부

GONE ARE THE DAYS
그때 그 시절

엇박자

세월,
낮이라고 다 낮이 아닌
밤이라고 다 밤이 아닌
그런 세월이 있지요.

인생의 중천에서
자갈길 엇박자 삶은 턱까지 숨차도
한낮엔 희끄무레한 잠을 자고
밤이면 발끝으로 삶을 굴리며

외발자전거
헐레벌떡 앞만 보고 달릴 때
하늘 향한 머리는 오히려 꼿꼿하고
비췻빛 청정한 꿈이 하도 푸르러
한오백년처럼 멀고 푸르러

세월,
별이 떴다고 다 밤이 아니던
해가 떴다고 다 낮이 아니던
그래요!
그런 세월 하나 내게도 있었지요.

Offbeat

Time:
There is such a Time
That daytime does not always mean day time
Nor does nighttime mean night time either.

In settler's heydays
When life was rough on the offbeat
Having a whitish sleep during the days
Tiptoeing in the marketplace of living at nights,

Yet, pedalling a unicycle mightily;
Eyes kept watching straight forward
Head held high towards the sun, for
Blue dreams seemed so clear and promising
And Time would stay forever young with me.

Time:
There once was such a Time:
Neither starry sky meant nighttime
Nor sunny sky meant daytime either.
Yes, I have been there!

이민(移民) 첫 번지

옷 가방 하나
책가방 하나
이민자 유출 허용금 2백 달러*
천도 빛 나의 심장이
이민의 첫 담금질 당하던 곳
오크 8가(街)*

그라우스 산(山) 능선 위로
저녁놀 낭자할 때면
못 견디는 향수(鄕愁)와
무릎 빠지는 외로움을
오래된 사랑니의 통증처럼
말없이 눈물로 견뎌야 하던 곳

온종일 구겨진 희망이란 단어
밤마다 희미한 형광등 불빛에 다림질해 펴도
날이 밝으면 찾아가 두드려야 했던
수많은 문 앞에서
두려움은 늘 용기를 가로막고

내 작은 창가에 저녁별 기웃거리면
길 건너 '보우-맥' 네온사인 불빛에도
목울대 아프게 차오르던 그리움은
어머니…
어머니…

뿌리째 뽑혀와 낯선 땅에 두 발 묻고
맨살의 어깻죽지 뼛속까지 시리던
한 인생 접목의 계절
나의 이민 첫 번지.

[노트] 오크 8가(街): Oak Street and 8th Avenue, Vancouver: 1970년 겨울, 내가
캐나다 밴쿠버에 도착하여 이민의 첫 여장을 푼 곳. 그 무렵 우연하게도 한국인
이민자 몇 가구가 Oak & 8th Avenue 주변에 모여와 이민의 고락을 함께 나누며
살았다.

First Address of Immigration

One suitcase of clothes
One suitcase of books
*Two hundred dollars cash allowed for immigrants,
My young heart took the first step
Into the hardship of an immigrant life
At Oak Street & 8th Avenue*.

When evening−glow spread puddle of bright red
Over the Grouse Mountain ridge,
The unbearable nostalgia
And the deep loneliness
I had to endure silently in tears
Like the pain of an old wisdom−tooth.

Even though I ironed out my crumpled hopes
In the dim fluorescent light every night,
The next day
In front of the doors that I had to knock
Fear of rejection always hindered my courage.

When the evening stars visited my tiny window,
Even the 'Bow—Mac' neon sign across the street
Made me choke with welling up longing for you,
Mother···
Mother···

Uprooted and transplanted to the foreign land,
Bare shoulders were cold to the bone.
The season of a life grafting
The first address of my immigration.

[Note] Oak Street & 8th Avenue: The first place I arrived and started my immigrant's life in Vancouver, Canada, the winter of 1970. Around that time, several Korean new immigrant families happened to live around that area, Oak & 8th Avenue, and shared the joys and sorrows of immigration.

높고 두꺼운 벽들

밴쿠버엔 이루 다 셀 수 없이 많은 문이 있는데, 새로 온 이민자들에게는 왜 그다지도 고집스럽게 열리지 않는 걸까? 미지의 세계를 열어가는 여정은 어쩌자고 이토록 살얼음판 걷는 것처럼 위태롭고 두려운 걸까?

저 높고 두꺼운 하얀 벽들, 그 뒤에 숨죽인 수많은 문들–

스스로 택한 더 나은 제2의 인생을 만나기 위해 오늘도 온종일 애타게 문들을 두드리고 다닌 나의 손은 아프고 지쳤다.

검은 망토를 걸친 저녁이 점령군처럼 밀려오고, 남편이 도시락 주머니 들고 야간 근무하러 집을 나가면, 동그마니 홀로 남은 나는 어쩔 수 없이 한밤중 거대한 어둠의 정적 속에 홀로 떠는 외로운 별–

지극히 작은 소리에도 나는 생쥐처럼 깜짝깜짝 놀라며 두려움에 떤다. 밤은 우리 위층 히피족 청년이 아편에 취해 내뱉는 괴성 사이로 흠칫흠칫 소스라치며 깊어 가는데…

아, 어머니

이런 밤엔 당신 계신 곳이 갑절로 먼 듯합니다!

[노트] 1971년 12월, 밴쿠버에서의 두 번째 겨울. 한국에서 약사였던 남편은 캐나다에서 좀처럼 본인의 전공 직업을 찾을 수 없었다. 그는 이곳 BCIT의 금속공학과에 등록할 때까지 거의 2년 가까이 야간 건물 청소부로 일했다.

The High and Thick Walls

There are so many doors to count in Vancouver, yet why are they so stubborn to open for new immigrants? Why the journey through unknown world is so uneasy and scary like walking on thin ice?

The high and thick white walls; The silent doors behind the walls. In order to meet a better 2nd life I chose, my hands are weary from knocking on the doors all day.

When the evening in his black cloak rushes in like an occupying force, and my husband goes to work the *graveyard shift, carrying his lunch box, I am all alone in the middle of the night, trembling like a lone star deep of the core of stillness in the dark immensity.

I skitter and jumpy after every slight noise like a scary little mouse. The night fright deepens between the ecstatic screams of the young hippie man in the suite right above ours, doped on marijuana—

Oh, Mother

On such nights, you seem twice far away!

[Note] Dec. 1971, my second winter in Vancouver. My husband who was a pharmacist in Korea, couldn't find a job in his profession in Canada. So, he worked as a night shift janitor for almost 2 years until he enrolled in BCIT, and took Chemical and Metallurgical Technology.

빈처(貧妻)의 일기

진창에다 맨발이어도 괜찮아
창창한 미래가 내 눈앞에 보이니까
손수건만 한 창문으로는
별빛 한 줄기 들일 수 없다 해도
별것 아냐, 참을 수 있어.
비록 우리의 가까운 미래는 불확실해도
삶의 쟁반 마주 든 한 사람과
기댈 수 있는 그의 따뜻한 등만 있으면 됐지.
비록 K. 양로병원의 고단한 노동에
물집 잡힌 손끝이어도
계속 꿈을 길어 올리는 나의 가슴이면 됐지.
은하수 저편에서
조심조심 날개 달고 있는
꿈만 접지 말아 준다면
안개 낀 들판을 건너
아주 천천히 내게로 오고 있는
푸른 내일만 막지 말아 준다면.

[노트] 1973년, 남편은 BCIT 학생이었고, 나는 K 양로병원에서 1년간 간병인으로 일했다.

Diary of a Poor Man's Wife

Though I am barefoot on a muddy road, it's okay
because I see the bright future spread before me.
Though my window is as small as a handkerchief,
not one streak of starlight gets through it,
it's not a big deal, for I will bear it.
Even if our immediate future looks unsure,
he, who carries the Tray−of−Life with me,
and his warm back for me to lean on is all I need.
Even if my fingertips are blistered
from the hard work in the K. Private Hospital,
my heart keeps drawing undying dreams.
Just do not fold away the wing−of−dreams
that is getting ready carefully
at the other side of the Milky Way.
Just do not block the hope−of−tomorrow
that is coming toward me ever so slowly
across from the foggy fields.

[Note] Winter of 1973, my husband was studying at BCIT, and I was working
for the K. Private Hospital as a caregiver for a year.

어머니, 당신의 딸이 첫 아이를 낳았어요

고운 수선화들이 환하게 웃음 터뜨리는 3월
드디어 새 생명 하나 내 품에 안겼다.
 "예쁜 아가야, 네 아빠는 오늘도 학교에 가셨다.
  동생처럼 어린 학우들 사이에서
  이민의 땅에 우리의 미래를 건설하느라
  지금 열심히 공부하고 계신다."

옆 침대들이 축하객들의 꽃다발로 둘러싸일 때
나는 우리 아기에게 어쩐지 미안했다
우리 침대에만 꽃이 없는 게 내 탓이기라도 한 듯.

우리 아기의 탄생을 알리는 기쁜 소식은
열흘쯤 뒤에 고향 사람들에게 전달되겠지만,
태평양 건너편 나의 어머니는
미역국을 끓여다 주시기엔 너무나 멀리 계신다.
 "어머니, 기뻐하세요!
  당신의 딸이 어제 첫아들을 낳았어요
  건강하고 예쁜 당신의 첫 외손주여요. 그런데
  저는 왜 자꾸만 눈물이 나나요, 어머니?"

[노트] 1974년 봄, 첫아들 A가 밴쿠버 Grace Children's Hospital에서 태어났다.

Mother, Your Daughter Gave Birth to First Child

In March when sweet daffodils smile brightly,
A new life finally arrived in my arms.
  "Sweet baby, your dad had to go to the school
  Studying hard along with the classmates who
  Are as young as his younger siblings
  To build our future in the land of immigration."

When the neighboring beds surrounded with flowers,
I felt guilty to my baby, as if it were my fault
Not having flower bouquets on our table.

Though news of our baby's arrival will be delivered
To the folks in my hometown in about ten days,
My mother across the Pacific Ocean is
Too far away to bring me seaweed−soup.
  "Rejoice, Dear mother!
  Your daughter gave birth to first boy yesterday.
  Your first grandchild, healthy and beautiful, but why
  Tears stream down on my cheeks like this, Mother?"

[Note] spring of 1974, my first son A. was born at the Grace Children's Hospital in Vancouver.

옛날 옛적 그 겨울밤

춥고 바람 몹시 불던 밤이었어
남편과 아이는 기침약에 취해서
곤히 잠이 들고
나 혼자 앉아서 학년말 시험 공부하는데
기침과 고열로 온몸이
불덩어리 되어 떨었지

　덜컹⋯ 덜컹⋯
삭풍에 유리창 밤새 울고
잦은 기침은 독풀처럼 나의 목을 할퀴었지만
행여라도 약에 취해 잠들면 어쩌나
온밤을 진저리치며
생으로 고통을 참아야 했지

한 차례 줄기침 끝에
불현듯 눈앞에 난무하던 별들과
열에 뜬 나의 손바닥 위로
뚝뚝 듣던 새빨간 액체들
지는 장미의 마지막 비명같이 처연한
꽃잎⋯ 꽃잎⋯ 꽃잎⋯

이민의 땅 프레이저강* 강가에서
천 년 살 듯 만 년 살 듯
혼신으로 대들보를 끌어 올리며
아플 때 약 먹고 곰처럼 잠자는
남편과 어린 아들이 세상에서 가장 부럽던
옛날 옛적 그 겨울밤.

[노트] 1975년 1월, 내가 밴쿠버 커뮤니티 칼레지(VCC) 치과 기술사 4년 과정의
2년 차 때 이야기.

Once Upon a Winter Night

Cold and windy was the night.
My husband and little baby fell asleep,
One in the bed and one in the baby crib,
Drunk from the cough medicine.
Beside them, I sat, coughing and shivering
In high fever, studying for the final-term exam.

clatter... clatter...
The window rattled incessantly.
My throat pained as if pricked by poison ivy,
But for a fear of falling asleep,
I refused to take the cough syrup;
Endured the pain throughout the night.

After a bad coughing spell,
Hundreds of stars rained down before my eyes
And there, onto my feverish palms,
Bright red droplets started to fall:
Pitiful, like screaming of last rose petals;
Petal… petal… petal…

As if I would live for thousand years,

Building a future in the land of immigration

By the Fraser River*,

How I envied my husband and little son, sleeping

Like drunken bears after taking their medicine,

Once upon a time, one winter night.

[Note] Jan. 1975, on my second year of the Four-year-Dental Technician Course, VCC.

어느 비 내리는 오후

I
어느 비 내리는 오후였단다
나는 늘 그랬던 것처럼
2층 미세스 킴 네 아파트를 향하여
두 계단씩 뛰어 올라갔어
얼마나 기다리던 순간이던가
정확과 정밀의 치과 기술사 공부에 온종일 바빴지만
이른 아침에 미세스 킴 손에 맡기고 온
두 살짜리 네가 한 순간이라도 뇌리에서 떠난 적 있을까
오, 얼마나 간절히 그리워했던가
내 품에 너를 보듬어 안고
젖 먹이고 기저귀 갈아주고 자장가 불러주는
지극히 간단하면서도 아름다운
여느 엄마들의 평범한 일상의 일들을─

II
나는 급히 문을 두드렸어
미세스 킴이 문을 열어주었지 그녀는
너와 동갑내기 아들 유진이를 품에 안고 있었어
그리고 미세스 킴의 바로 뒤에 네가 서 있더구나
한 손에는 우유병을 들고
다른 손에는 장난감 토끼의 귀를 거머잡고서─
우리의 눈이 마주치자 너의 입술이 씰룩댔어
그리고 너는 곧 울음을 터뜨렸지

그건 오직 아이의 엄마만 이해할 수 있는
너무도 많은 말을 포함한 울음이었어
기쁨과 불만이 온통 뒤범벅된
두 살배기가 할 수 있는 유일한 표현 방법이었지.

Ⅲ
사랑하는 아들아, 너는 모르리!
그날 너를 자동차에 태우고 집으로 돌아오며
내가 얼마나 흐느껴 울었는가를—
유진이가 제 엄마의 품에 안겨 젖을 빨 때
너는 네 손으로 우유병을 들고 빨면서
얼마나 유진이를 부러워했을까
그걸 상상하며
오, 내 가슴 얼마나 찢어질 듯 아팠던가를—
나는 학교도 미래도 꿈도 다 접고
당장 내 아기의 전임 엄마로 집에 들어앉고 싶었어
사십오 년 전의 비 내리던 그날 오후에는.

[노트] 1976년 여름, 나의 VCC 덴탈 테크니션 4년 과정 중 3년 차 어느 날.

One Rainy Afternoon

I

One rainy afternoon it was.

I ran up the stairs,

two steps at a time as usual,

to the Kim's suite on the second floor.

How I waited for that moment.

While busy learning and practicing

the dental technic, accuracy and precision, yet,

never a moment had I forgotten my two−year−old boy

I left in the hands of Mrs. Kim every early morning.

Oh, how much I missed to hold you and feed you,

change your diapers and sing you to sleep−

the simplest yet most beautiful daily chores

those mothers do for their babies.

II

I knocked on the door hurriedly;

Mrs. Kim opened the door, carrying in her arms,

her own baby boy Eugene, the same age as you.

And you were standing behind Mrs. Kim,

holding your milk bottle in one hand and

a toy bunny−rabbit by the ear in the other hand.

As soon as our eyes met, your lips quivered,

and before long, you let out a cry.

A cry that meant much more than a cry−
an expression of joy and grievance−
the only way two−year−old boy knew
and only his mother understood so well.

Ⅲ

Dear Son, you would never know.
On our way home, you in the baby seat at the back,
I sobbed and cried hard;
Imagining,
how you must have envied Eugene tenderly nursed
from his mother's breast while you were holding
and sucking your own milk bottle in your hand.
Oh, the pain of guilt and remorse I had to suffer!
I wanted to quit school, future, and dream immediately;
and stay home as a full−time−mom to my baby,
that rainy afternoon of four−and−half decades ago.

[Note] summer of 1976, my 3rd year of the Dental Technician Course at Vancouver Community College(VCC).

내가 아닌 것들로

세상은
세상이 아닌 것들로
세상이 되었네요
너, 나, 그…

꽃은
꽃이 아닌 것들로
꽃이 되었고요
태양, 구름, 바람…

나는
내가 아닌 것들로
내가 되었어요
꿈, 기도, 그리움…

첫눈 앞세우고 겨울은 왔지만
한 뼘 밑 흙 속에 봄이 있지요
내일에 내일이 오면
꽃도 다시 핀다고 해요

그래서 오늘도
여기 세상 속을
내가 살아가고 있네요
내가 아닌 것들로

[**노트**] 이 시는 2002년에 쓰고, 그 후 여러 행사에서 영어와 한국어로 낭송되어 그때마다 많은 이들의 찬사를 받았다. 2008년 WPRS의 5개국 시인들의 시(詩)와 함께 Co-Op 라디오 쇼에서 낭송, 2012년 유네스코의 '세계 모국어의 날' 행사에서 낭송 등.

As an Inter-Being* of Many a Non-I

The world
Became the world
By interconnecting many a non−world:
You, I, they⋯

The flower
Became the flower
By interconnecting many a non−flower:
The sun, the clouds, the wind⋯

And I
Became the I
By interconnecting many a non−I:
Dreams, prayers, yearnings⋯

Though the winter rushes in shortly after the first snow,
Three inches deep in the earth, the spring awaits.
The flowers will bloom again
When tomorrow's tomorrow comes.

So, here I am
Living today
In this world
As an Inter−being* of many a non−I.

[Note] This poem was written in 2002, and has been recited in English and Korean at various events and praised by many people: Recited on the Co-Op radio show(2008); recited at the UNESCO event 'the International Mother Language Day'(2012); etc.

초록 약속

한겨울 불모의 땅에서도
내가 꿈을 포기하지 못하는 것은
멀리서 천천히 오고 있는
당신의 초록 약속을
믿기 때문입니다
창틀에 걸터앉은 2월 어린 햇살 편에
그대 잊지 않고 전해주시는
가슴 뛰는 기쁜 소식:
"기다려라, 조금만 더 기다려라
절망하지 말아라
이제 곧 봄이 온다
어제는 오늘의 어머니
오늘은 내일을 잉태하고
내일 우리는 노래 부르리니."
겨우내 잠자던 나의 시혼(詩魂)은
당신의 초록 둥지에서
봄마다 다시 깨어나고
비상을 꿈꾸는 하얀 날개 한 쌍
내 안에 뜨겁게 날아오를 것을
나, 확실히 믿기 때문입니다.

The Green Promise

Though winter barren land is desolate,
I do not give up my dream
Because I believe;
Your green promise is coming slowly
From far yonder.
Young February sunlight sits on my windowsill
Conveys your glad message to me
And my heart palpitates with a joy:
  "Wait. Wait a little longer.
  Despair not,
  For spring is just around the corner.
  Yesterday is mother of today;
  Today conceives tomorrow;
  Tomorrow we will sing."
Because I certainly believe that
In the green nest of yours
My dormant hopes revive every spring,
And the spirit of poetry rises in me
On her pair of white wings
With a burning desire of a flight.

프레이저강의 나비들

우울한 날엔
프레이저 강둑에 나가곤 했어요.
들장미 넝쿨들 지나
붉은 뗏목들의 긴 기다림 넘어
은빛 윤슬나비*들 현란하게 팔랑거리는
프레이저 푸른 강물 줄기를 만났어요.

어제와 오늘의 온갖 근심 걱정의 무게와
내일 넘어야 할 험산 준령의 두려움은
반짝이는 윤슬나비들 날갯짓에 날아가 버려
훌훌 벗겨져 날아가 버려
내 마음 새털처럼 가벼워지곤 했어요.

마음이 길 잃고 우울할 때
프레이저 강둑에 서서
팔랑거리며 흐르는 윤슬나비들을 바라보고 있으면
먼데 나의 꿈 한 발짝 다가오는 듯하고
닿을 수 없는 영혼의 그리움도
내일의 약속 쪽으로 길을 내어주곤 했어요.

여기 프레이저 강둑에서는 모든 것이
충만하고 아름다웠어요.
삶의 욕망이 다시 한번 가슴에 용솟음쳤고
마음은 활짝 즐거워지곤 했어요.
내가 바로 로터스랜드*에서 노래 부르는
행복한 오월의 여왕인 양 느껴지곤 했어요.

[노트] 햇빛이나 달빛에 반짝이는 잔물결을 '윤슬'이라 하는데, 햇빛 좋은 날이면
프레이저 강 잔물결이 마치 은빛 나비들이 팔랑거리는 것처럼 보이므로 나는 그
것을 '윤슬나비'라고 부른다.

Butterflies of the Fraser River

Whenever I felt blue,
I came to the Fraser riverbank.
Past the stretch of wild−rose bushes
Behind the red timbers long waiting
I met the blue belt of the Fraser River
Fluttering like a flock of sparkling silver butterflies;

Weight of anxieties and worries of yesterday and today
And fear of mountains I have yet to climb tomorrow,
All lifted and blown away with the wind
By the Yoonseul−butterflies[*] sparkling flutter
And my heart felt as light as a feather.

When I felt lost and melancholy,
I came to the Fraser riverbank and
Watched the fluttering Yoonseul−butterflies,
My faraway songs seemed to come up one step closer
And the unreachable longing of my soul, too, drew near
Towards the promising morrow.

Here on the bank of the Fraser River,

All was abundant and beautiful;

Surges of life arose anew in my heart once again

Made me rejoice and delightful;

I felt like myself a happy queen of May

Singing in the Lotusland*.

[Note] Yoonseul(윤슬) means sparkling ripples in the moonlight or sunlight in Korean. Because the ripples of the Fraser River in the sunlight looks like fluttering silver butterflies, I call the ripples 'Yoonseul Butterflies'

내 안의 속삭임

내가 눈빛 맑은 소녀일 적에
나의 아버지는 늘 내게 말씀하셨네.
 "무엇을 하든 언제나 네 최선을 다하거라
  포기하지 말아라, 천 리 길도 한 발짝부터니라."

내가 뺨 붉고 꿈 많은 처녀가 되었을 때
나의 어머니는 몸소 행동으로 보여주셨네.
 "꿈을 지닌 여자는 울지 않는다
  더 열심히 일하고 더 오래 기다린다."

내가 '이민'이라는 쪽배를 타고 거친 파도에 휩쓸릴 때
혹은, 나의 꿈이 삶의 장터에서 길 잃고 헤맬 때
나를 넘어지지 않고 버티게 해준 것은
어릴 적에 들려주신 내 아버지의 말씀이었네.

세월이 나도 모르게 내 곁을 흘러가고
꽃들은 저희끼리 번갈아 다녀갔는데
뒤늦게 옛 꿈을 찾아 나선 나
이제는 가슴 깊은 곳 내 어머니의 속삭임을 듣네.
 "꿈을 지닌 여자는 울지 않는다.
  더 열심히 노력해라, 네 꿈이 널 찾아올 때까지.
  그땐, 마음껏 힘껏 노래하거라.
  그리하여 네 꿈을, 그리고 네 운명을, 완성하거라."

[노트] 이 시는 '밴쿠버 타고르 협회 시(詩) 공모전, 2018'의 수상작품들 중 하나이
며, 시상식에서 낭송하였음.

56

Whisper from Deep Within

When I was a little girl with sparkling eyes,
My father used to say to me:
  "Whatever you do, always do your best.
  Don't quit; a thousand−Li* begins with a single step."

When I grew as a rosy lass with budding dreams,
My mother always showed me in actions:
  "Dreaming girls don't cry;
  They work harder and wait patiently."

It was my father's words that kept me going
When life was abrasive in the vessel, "Immigration"
Pushed and pulled fiercely in its flow
And my dream got lost in the marketplace of Living.

Time has rushed by me unchecked
Flowers have come and gone unnoticed
I am now looking for my long−lost dream
And I hear my mother's whisper from deep within:
  "Dreaming girls don't cry;
  Work harder still until your dream finds you.
  And then, sing aloud heart and soul;
  Thus fulfill your dream; Thus fulfill your Destiny."

[Note] One of the winners of 'The Vancouver Tagore Society Poetry Contest 2018', and read at the Award Ceremony.

어느 한국산 향나무의 자서전

스물다섯 살 한국산 향나무였소 나는
싹 트는 푸른 꿈 한 아름 안고서
해마다 보릿고개*를 힘겹게 넘던 모국을 뒤로하고
바다 건너 먼 이국땅에 옮겨와 심어졌소
키 큰 삼나무들 사이에서 마음은 위축되었어도
태양 향해 머리 꼿꼿이 들고
새 뿌리에 새 가지 혼신으로 뻗으며
허리 펴고 푸른 향내 품는 일 쉽지 않았소

그립다고 어찌 다 말로 하리까
그리운 고향 산천 가슴 깊이 묻어 두고
가시덤불 후미진 타향의 에움길에서
명치 끝에 잠든 꿈 사르고 또 사를 때
포기하지 않았소; 절망은 금물이었소!

나도 모르게 세월은 흐르고—참 빨리도 흐르고…
이제는 나이 든 한국산 향나무
굳은살에 옹이들 훈장인 양 주렁주렁 달고서
여기 단풍잎의 나라*를 제2의 조국이라 부르며 사오
고향 떠나 멀리 또 하나의 고향을 이루어
살붙이고 정들인 곳
밴쿠버, 아름다운 로터스랜드에서.

Biography of A Korean Incense-Juniper

A twenty−five−year−old Korean−incense−juniper was I,
With sprouting green dreams, left mother country where
White−clad folk had to pass barley−hump* every year,
And transplanted to the foreign land across the Ocean.
Though feeling small among tall cedar trees,
Head held high upright toward the sun,
Took new roots and branches all my might, while
Embracing the evergreen scent; it wasn't easy at all.

How can I put into words that how much I missed!−
My sweet old hometown buried deep in my heart.
It was very hard to rekindle the dormant dreams within
On the trail of thorn−bushes in the strange land,
Yet, I neither given up, nor despaired.

Without noticing it, time flew by− flew by very fast!
Now the aged Korean−Incense−Juniper
With calluses and knots all over like medallions,
Calling the *Maple−Leaf−Country:
"My Second Homeland"
Settled and cared a new home far away from home
Here in Vancouver the beautiful Lotusland

Part Two
제2부

THE COLOURS OF A LIFE
삶의 색깔들

달걀부침꽃

I

내 나이 여섯 혹은 일곱 살일 때, 나의 어머니는
레그혼 닭 다섯 마리 기르신 적 있다
수탉 한 마리 암탉 네 마리
닭들은 어머니의 정성에 보답하듯
열심히 알을 낳았다
하루에 한 알
어떤 날은 두 알
알들은 고스란히
부엌 살강 위 함지박에 모여졌다

매주 월요일 아침마다
우리 집 밥상은 온통
하얗고 노란 꽃밭이었다
어머니의 달걀부침꽃들-
밥그릇마다 한 송이씩 올라앉아서
맛있게 웃던 그 꽃들을
나는 밥 한 그릇을 다 먹을 때까지
아주 조금씩 아끼며 맛있게
베어 먹곤 했다

Ⅱ
삶이여,
사랑이여,
나는 그대들을
오래전 그 달걀부침 꽃처럼
아주 소중히 아끼며 먹고 있다

일생이라는 밥그릇에 남아 있는
많지 않은 내 앞 세월임을
잘 알기에
마지막 한 방울의 시간을 삼키는
그 숭고한 순간까지
나는 그대들을 아껴 먹을 것이다

왜 진작에 몰랐을까?
이 맛을—
이 소중함을—
이따금 가슴 찡한 느낌표도
소금 찍듯이 찍으며
맛있게!
아주 맛있게!

Fried-Egg-Flowers

I

When I was six or seven,
My mother raised five Leghorn chickens:
A rooster and four hens.
They laid eggs diligently
As mother took good care of them.
One egg a day
Or two on some days
Mother collected them
In the wooden basket on the kitchen shelf.

On every Monday morning,
Our breakfast table became a flowerbed
Of yellow and white—
My mother's fried—egg—flowers.
One flower on top of each rice bowl
Smiled deliciously.
I ate them small bite at a time
Enjoying each and every bite
Until I finished the whole bowl of rice.

Ⅱ

Dear Life

Dear Love

I am enjoying you each small bite

Just like the fried−egg−flowers

I ate a long time ago.

Knowing

Not much Time left,

I will cherish you evermore

Until the sacred moment I swallow

The last drop of Time

From my hourglass.

Why hadn't I known it sooner

This taste−

This preciousness−

From time to time

I put exclamation marks

As if dipping salt on my fried eggs

Deliciously!

Oh, so deliciously!

조각보 이불 1
–삶의 색깔들

내 앞에 펼쳐진 *조각보 이불을 본다
형형색색 헝겊 조각들로 만들어진 모습
그렇게 아우러져 온
내 삶의 순간들을 똑 닮았다
하얀색: 순수와 순결의 상징
이마도 나 이 세상에 태어나던 날
제일 먼저 내 알몸을 감쌌을 흰 무명 포대기
내 나이 스물다섯 살 때 입었던 웨딩드레스
검은색: 죽음과 어둠의 신비
아마도 나 이 세상 하직하는 날
다 벗고 가는 내 영혼에 볼 비벼주고
나와 함께 이승의 강을 건널 마지막 색
그리고는 일곱 가지 무지개 색깔:
행복, 기쁨, 슬픔, 분노, 평화, 희망, 꿈
이룬 것들, 이루지 못한 것들
잠시 옆으로 비켜 놓았다가 영영 잊고만 것들
어깨와 어깨 마주 대고 꿰매어져
알록달록, 한 장 이불 되어 펼쳐진
내 생애–
조각보 이불.

Applique Quilt 1
−The Colours of a Life

An *applique quilt spread in front of me
A patchwork of colourful fabrics
Sewn together piece by piece
That resembles the moments of my life.
White patches: symbol of innocence and purity.
Perhaps the colour of the cotton sheet that wrapped
My naked body at the time I arrived in This World,
And the wedding dress I wore at twenty−and−five.
Black patches: symbol of death and dark mystery.
Probably the last colour that will kiss my naked soul
And crosses the river of This Life with me
When my time comes to an end.
And then, the colours of a rainbow:
Happy, joy, sorrow, anger, peace, hope, and dream.
Some things succeeded and some didn't.
Some were put aside, then forgotten forever.
Stitched shoulder to shoulder
Laid out as one colourful quilt:
My life−
An applique quilt.

조각보 이불 2
–한 땀 한 땀 인연의 실올로

제 하늘 품고
제 노래 부르던
제 다른 꽃 가슴들이었다
포기할 수 없는
절망할 수도 없는
아직도 선연한 무지갯빛 꿈들일레
시침질로 감침질로
알록달록 손잡고 함께 달려왔다

삶이란 수수께끼 세상 속의 끈질긴 행진
요지경 속을 헤치고 헤쳐 길 만들기
미지의 내일을 향해 경작해 나가는 것

아픈 이마 서로 짚어주고
무거운 짐 서로 들어주며
얼굴에 얼굴 맞대고
가슴에 가슴 붙이고
한 땀 한 땀 인연의 실올로 꿰매어져서
서리서리 보듬고 오늘을 산다
굽이굽이 한마당 인생을 산다

Applique Quilt 2
—Stich by stitch with karmic threads

Different skies

Different songs

In different blossoming hearts.

Neither giving up

Nor despaired

For dreams still there in vivid rainbow colours.

Tack on sometimes, darn in other times

Hand—in—hand, every dappled moment.

Life is a tenacious march amid the enigmatic world

Making a way through a kaleidoscope

Plowing forward to the unknown morrow.

Caring for each other

Helping one another

Face to face

Heart to heart

Stitch by stitch with karmic threads

Together embrace and shape, living today.

Together one sheet of life, living a destiny.

감사합니다!

세상일 늘 맘과 같이 쉽지 않아서
불만과 후회의 날들도 더러 있지만
그래도 여전히 감사한 것들이 많아서
나는 오늘도 감사한 마음으로 살아갑니다.

오늘 새벽 동쪽 지평선에서 꿈틀대며 날아오른
찬란한 주홍빛 태양을 보아준
나의 두 눈에 감사하고
지난밤 풀벌레들의 푸른 합창을 들어준
나의 두 귀에 감사합니다.

달리고, 호흡하고, 소화하고
그 외 보이지도 느끼지도 못하는 여러 일로
나를 지금 여기에 살아 있게 하는
나의 심장, 폐, 위장, 그리고
내 살 속의 모든 장기와 세포들에도 감사합니다.

온종일 환한 세상 어디쯤서 분주하다가
하루 끝엔 제 둥지로 모여드는
세 아들의 젊은 가족들에 감사하고
지금 '감사합니다'라는 이 시를 쓰고 있는
여기 나 자신에게도 감사합니다.

또 한 가지 아주 중요한 것 있습니다.
지난 50년을 한결같이
인생이라는 같은 배를 나와 함께 노 저어 온
한 사람의 세월 묻은 두 손에
진심으로 감사합니다!

Thank You!

Though worldly things are not as easy as we want,
And there are days of dissatisfaction and regret,
I live with a grateful heart today because
There are still many things yet to be thankful for.

I thank my eyes for seeing
The splendid orange sun wriggling out
From the eastern horizon this morning.
I thank my ears for listening
To the crickets' green chorus last night.

I thank my lungs, heart, and stomach
And the rest of all the organs and cells
For breathing, running, and digesting.
And other services, though unaware and unseen,
Those keep me alive here and now.

I thank my children's families for busy themselves
In their bright world all day, and returning safely
To their nests at the end of each day.
And also, I thank myself for being here and now,
Writing this poem "Thank You".

There is one more very important thing;

I am truly grateful

For the time—stained hands of one person

Who has been rowing the same boat, Life, with me

All along for the past 50 years!

미안해요

잡힐 듯 잡힐 듯
달아나는 시어(詩語)들
온종일 키보드 위에서 술래잡기하다가
이 저녁도
초특급 행 밥상이 차려졌네요.
당신 좋아하는 해물탕 재료
생조기와 생새우는
아직도 냉동고에 얼린 채이고
멸치조림, 구운 김, 신 김치와 된장국
또 식탁에 올렸네요.
오늘 아침엔 양말 서랍이 텅텅 비어서
말없이 빨래건조기에서 꺼내어 신는 것
안 보는 척 뺨 붉히며
곁눈질로 보았지요.
돈도 밥도 안 되는
시 나부랭이 쓰는 아내 둔 불편함
말 않는 그 속이야 오죽하련만
미안해요,
정말 미안해요!

I Am Sorry

As if to be caught, as if to be caught,
And yet the words keep fleeing away.
I played hide−and−seek with poetic words
On the keyboard all day, then ended up
Serving a speedy dinner this evening again.
The yellow−croaker fish and raw shrimps−
Your favorite seafood soup ingredients−
Still in the deep−freezer; Seasoned anchovies and
Seaweed roast, sour kimchi and miso soup
Were put on the dinner table instead.
When the socks−drawer was empty this morning,
You quietly took a pair from the dryer and put them on.
I looked at you with a side glance and blushed,
Pretending, I did not see it.
Neither money nor bread my poems bring home,
Yet you never say a word about the inconvenience
Of having a poet−wife−
I am sorry,
I am truly sorry!

가다가 숨차면

이순(耳順) 언덕 넘어
고희(古稀) 산 중턱
가다가 숨차고 어지럽거든
큰 숨 들이쉬고 잠시 쉬어가거라.
허리 펴고 이마에 땀 닦으며 바라보면
어제 놓친 시어들이
치자 빛 노을 속에 모여 앉아서
가을 색깔로 물결치고 있잖니.
이따금 사랑도 지쳐 아픔이 따르고
가슴 시린 억새밭에 고독이 서걱대도
아직 펼쳐 보지 않은 내일의 어느 갈피엔
혼자라도 지켜야 할 약속이 기다리고 있거늘
곧 해가 진다고 하여도 돌아서지 말아라.
가슴 방엔 아직도 못다 부른 노래가 남아 있고
세월 전 꽃잎처럼 잊은 듯 잊힌 듯
그리움 달빛 속으로 하얗게 길을 가나니
여인아!
가다가 몹시 숨차고 어지럽거든
산 중턱 검바위 발치에 앉아서
개밥바라기별 눈썹 위에 걸어놓고
이 잠시 쉬어가거라.

If You Are Out of Breath

Over the hill of Sixtieth,

On the mountain slope of Seventieth,

If you are out of breath and feeling dizzy,

Take a deep breath and rest a little while.

Stretch, and wipe your forehead and look;

The poems you missed yesterday

Gathered there in the purple sunset-glow,

Rippling in autumn tint at the end of the day.

Love gets weary at times and pain may follow

And lonely heart is cold, rustles like pampas grass,

Yet, somewhere in the folds of unseen tomorrow,

A promise you have to keep is waiting for you.

Even if the sun will set soon, turn back not;

There are still songs to sing in your heart;

A yearning stretches white through the moonlight too,

As if forgot or be forgotten like flower petals of long ago.

O Woman!

If you are out of breath and feeling dizzy,

Sit by the mossy rock on the mountain slope

With the Evening Star hang above your eyebrow,

And then, take a rest a little while. Now.

안개꽃 레퀴엠

누가 울고 있는가
누구의 영혼이 흐느끼고 있는가
녹색 전봇대 그 밑동에 안개꽃 한 다발 놓여있다
아마도 미처 갈 채비 못 했던 영혼 하나가
황황히 먼 외길 떠났나보다

발밑 밝혀주는 연등도 없이
식어가는 손길 잡아주는 기도도 없이
마침표 찍는 소리 굉음으로 남기고
저 가는 곳도 미처 모르며
얼떨결에 총총히 떠났나보다

꽃 빛으로 벙글던 젊음이었을까
황혼길에 가슴 시리던 중년이었을까
죽은 이의 아픔을 통곡하는
어느 사랑하는 가슴이
안개꽃 한 다발로 울다 갔는가

비스듬히 누운 하얀 안개꽃 한 다발
그 위로
간 사람보다 더 조용하게
가랑비는 내리고.

A Bouquet of Requiem

Who is crying?
Whose soul is weeping?
At the base of the green electrical−pole
A bouquet of baby−breath is laid; Perhaps
A soul departed hurriedly for the road−of−no−return.

Without a Lotus Lantern lit under the feet,
Without comforting prayers for the cold hands,
With a confusion not knowing the destination,
With a crashing sound as the last period−mark,
Left this world in a hurry not even knowing where to.

Was it a youth with a blossoming heart?
Was it a middle−aged on a twilight−hill?
Whose sorrow−fed heart was there weeping
Upon for the painful departure, offering
A bunch of Baby−breath flower?

A bouquet of white tearful flowers laid at an angle
And there upon the white bouquet
The light rain is quietly falling down−
Even quieter than the dead one.

빼앗긴 악수(握手)
-COVID-19 펜데믹 1

악수요? 무슨 악수요?
제가 친구나 이웃들과 반갑게 나눈
마지막 악수가 언제였나요
이 무서운 코로나바이러스 전염병 창궐 이후
그건 *'팔꿈치 건드리기'로 대체되지 않았나요
팔꿈치 건드리기? 그게 무슨 말이죠?
친구를 만날 때 팔꿈치는 모든 신체 부위 중에서
가장 관심이 적게 가는 부분이 아니던가요
솔직히, 누가 타인의 팔꿈치에
관심을 두기나 했습니까?

전 세계가 다 함께 고통당하고 있는
이 끔찍한 공포의 시간 속에서
인간의 손들은 대책 없이 놓인 채
'악수' 같은 것은 애당초에 없는 듯, 악수를 피합니다
다정하게 손 마주 잡던 악수를 어디서 찾나요
마음 열어 얼싸안는 곰-포옹이 너무나도 그립습니다
오, 우주의 절대자여,
이제 인간들의 방종과 이기심의 죄를 제발 용서하시고
빼앗긴 악수와 곰-포옹을 돌려주십시오
부디, 하루속히 저희에게 돌려주십시오!

Stolen Handshakes
—COVID—19 Pandemic 1

Handshake? What handshake?
When was the last time I had a friendly handshake
with friends and neighbours?
Isn't it replaced by *elbow—touching
since the horrible Coronavirus arrived?
Elbow—touching? What's an elbow touching*?
Aren't elbows the least interesting parts
of all body parts, when one meets friends?
Earnestly, who has ever given much eye
to the elbows of another person.

At these horrific times of the COVID Pandemic,
the whole world suffers together.
Human hands are left unprepared helpless,
avoiding handshakes as if there has been no such thing.
Where do we find the friendly handshake?
I miss the heartfelt bear—hugs so much too.
O the Almighty of the Universe,
please forgive us for our indulgence and selfishness,
and give back our stolen handshake and bear—hug.
Would you please, give them back to us soon!

2020년 오월은 그렇게 오셨다
-COVID-19 펜데믹 2

해마다 오월은 오신다
새색시 고운 자태로 오신다
창포물에 머리 감아 빗고
아카시아꽃 하얀 버선발로
나비 날개에 사뿐히 얹혀 오신다

올해도 오셨다, 오월은
공포의 코로나바이러스도 아랑곳없이
싱그럽고 어여쁘게
따뜻하고 자애롭게
자비(慈悲)의 화신처럼 오신 님

방종과 이기심에 날뛴 벌(罰)로
코로나 팬더믹에 휩쓸려
온 세상이 다함께 허우적거릴 때
참회하는 가슴들을 용서하고 다독이며
안 보이지만 분명히 오월은 손길이 바쁘시다

"견디거라, 조금만 더 견뎌내거라
삶이란 가장 힘든 것을 견뎌내는 것이니라."

2020년의 오월은 그렇게 오셨다
연둣빛 숙고사 겹저고리 받쳐 입고
라일락 고운 향기 하늘가에 흩뿌리며
두려움에 떠는 영혼들을 위로하며 오셨다
눈물겹게, 오, 참으로 눈물겹게!

May of 2020 Came Thus
−COVID−19 Pandemic 2

Every year, May comes−
Comes as beautiful as a young newlywed wife.
Hair washed in iris−water and neatly combed,
Wearing white acacia flower socks,
Riding softly upon butterfly wings.

In spite of the horrific Coronavirus,
This year, too, May came;
Fresh and beautiful;
Warm and compassionate
Like an incarnation of the Goddess of Mercy.

When the whole world struggles
With the COVID Pandemic, being punished
For its self−indulgence and selfishness,
Unseen but certain, May is busy at work, forgiving
And caressing the repenting hearts−

"Be patient; Bear it a little longer.
Life is to endure the heaviest ordeal."

Thus, May of 2020 came;

Wearing a light-green silk Jeogori[*],

Spreading the sweet lilac scent in the air,

Comforting the souls those trembling in fear,

Touchingly. Oh, so touchingly!

[Note] Jeogori(저고리) is the traditional Korean basic upper garment for both men and women.

맨 아래 칸 서랍

요즘 골방 서랍장을 정리하는 날이 부쩍 늘었다.
놓지 못해 떠나지 못한 어제의 그림자들이
매미 허물같이 모여 사는 곳─,
돌쩌귀도 녹스는 늙은 세월에 대부분은 떠나고
몇은 아직 남아서 민속촌처럼 함께 저무는 그곳
늦가을 저녁의 체온 닮은 바람이 분다.
발돋움하던 별바라기의 풋 꿈도
이민의 자갈밭에 무시로 무릎 깨던 한낮도
사추(思秋)의 그리움 앓던 가을 여인의 갈증도
이제는 모두 치수 안 맞는 치마허린데
많은 것을 버리고도 끝내 못다 버려서
마음속 아래 칸 서랍에 묻어둔 것들
골고루 등 쓰다듬어 다시 누이고─
슬프디 한 내 그리움도 함께 누이고─
폐허 된 고향 집 문 닫아걸듯 쓸쓸히
다시 서랍장 문을 닫는다.
깊은 잠 방해받은 어제들이
신음하며 돌아눕는 소리 가슴으로 듣는다.

The Bottom Drawer

I organize the bottom drawer in my closet often lately.
In there, I see my yesterday's shadows that I could not
let go, gathered like cicadae skins.
As stone hinges rusted with time, most clothes are gone,
but some still remain like a folk−village, and getting older.
A chill wind blows there, resembling late autumn evenings.
The young stargazer's unsung dreams;
The settler's arduous midday on the gravel−roads;
The thirst of a woman in her autumnal longing;
Now all are but old clothes that waistlines fit no more!
Though many are thrown away, some are still buried
deep in the bottom drawer of my heart.
One by one, I pat them and gently lay them back again−
with them, my incurable melancholic longings too.
I close the drawer, feeling sad as if closing the door
of my dear old native home.
My heart hears moaning sound of the disturbed yesterdays
coming out of the closed bottom drawer.

망각의 샘물

마침내, 작은 나룻배 하나가 파란 별 동네 강가에 닿았다.

그와 그녀는 두 손을 꼭 잡은 채 '망각의 샘물' 앞에 서 있었다. 샘물엔 작고 하얀 표주박 하나 동동 떠 있고, 그들의 바로 옆에는 해와 달이 서로 머리 맞대고 서서 떠나는 그녀를 배웅하고 있었다.

새들이 일제히 손뼉을 쳤다. 꽃들은 낮은 목소리로 가장 아름다운 장송곡을 합창하기 시작했고, 세상의 종들은 조용조용 몸을 흔들어 강물 소리로 부드럽게 울었다.

"여보, 부디 잘 가오, 우리 다음 생(生)의 강가에서 꼭 다시 만납시다." 표주박으로 망각의 샘물을 떠올리는 그녀의 귀에 대고 그가 속삭였다.

"사랑하오." 그녀가 나룻배에 오르기 직전, 그가 황급히 한 마디 더 덧붙였지만, 그러나 그때 이미 표주박에서 마지막 한 모금의 샘물을 삼켜버린 그녀는 더는 그를 기억하지 못했다.

천천히 나룻배가 움직이기 시작했다. 남자가 그녀의 옷소매를 붙들며 섧디섧게 울었지만, 이제 그녀는 다만 갈 길이 먼 영혼의 길손일 뿐, 가슴에 두 손을 단정하게 모은 채 초점 없는 눈으로 강 건너 저쪽 피안(彼岸)의 해변을 향해 고요히 서 있었다.

이윽고, 강물 소리가 서서히 사라지고 꽃들은 이제 더는 노래를 부르지 않았다. 해와 달도 조용히 각각 저네들의 자리로 되돌아갔다.

Spring of Oblivion

Finally, a small ferry boat arrived on the river−shore of the Blue Star. In front of the Spring−of−Oblivion, he and she stood, holding each other's hand tightly. A tiny white gourd floated on the spring water, and very close to them, the Sun and the Moon stood head−to−head, to see her off.

All the birds clapped hands together. The flowers began to sing the most beautiful requiem, in a low tone, and all the bells in the world tolled softly in the sound of river−water.

"Goodbye, sweetheart. I'll meet you someday on the other shore." He whispered into her ears as she drew the water with the white gourd from the Spring−of−Oblivion.
"I love you." Hurriedly he added one more word just before she stepped into the ferryboat. But, by then, she who had already swallowed the last drop of the water from the white gourd, did not remember him anymore.

Slowly, the ferryboat began to move. He wept sorrowfully, clinging to her sleeves. But now she was just a wayfarer whose soul has a long way to go, standing quietly with her hands neatly folded on her chest, facing the shore at the world beyond across the river with unfocused eyes.

Before long, the sound of the river−water died down; And the flowers sang no more. The Sun and the Moon, too, quietly returned to where they belong.

Part Three
제3부

MY ISLAND
나의 섬

나의 섬

그제는 나의 마음 곳집에 혼불 살라 시(詩) 꽃 한 송이 피워 올리고, 어제는 마음 맞는 세계시인들 모아 시 꽃 잔치 한판 거나하게 벌이고, 영혼이 털털 비워 헛헛하고 쓸쓸한 오늘은 내 안의 나 만나러 나의 섬으로 갑니다. 아직 바깥에서 서성거리는 나를 불러들이고, 세상으로 난 문이란 문은 모두 닫아걸어 잠그고, 내 유배지의 하얀 밀실로 눅눅한 나의 영혼 벗어 말리러 갑니다.

고독이여— 나의 애인이여!

그대는 내 시(詩)들의 산실(産室)

그리움 타는 나의 영혼이 옷을 벗는

나만의 나, 절대 홀로의 섬입니다.

My Island

The day before yesterday, I burned my soul and bloom a poetry flower in the shrine of my heart. Yesterday, I threw a wild poetry party with fellow poets of the WPRS. When my soul is empty and feeling forlorn like today, I go to my island to meet my Inner Self. Call me in from outside, shut and lock all doors to the world, and go to the island, the white secret chamber of my exile, to take off my hollow and damp soul, and dry it.

O Solitude— My lover!

The birthplace of my poems

The Island of my Absolute Oneness

Where my yearning soul undresses.

편지
−나의 뮤즈에게 1

눈물과 함께
나의 노래를 띄웁니다.
차오르는 소망 싸서
기도와 함께 보냅니다.

가난한 나의 가슴 못에는
당신의 그림자가
어릴 적 우러르던 별들을 보듬은 채
아직도 그대로 잠겨 있습니다.

세월은
옛 이야기처럼 가고
아이는 먼 바다로 가서
외딴 섬이 되었지만

당신 향한 나의 꿈 나 아직 멈추지 않으렵니다
내 영혼의 뜨락에는
작고 소중한 불멸의 욕망 하나
노오란 민들레 꽃잎으로 피어 있기에.

[노트] 이 시의 영문버전「Letter」는 2003년 미국의 '국제 영문시 공모전'에서 편집부장상(賞)을 수상했음.

Letter
—To My Muse .1

I send my songs to you
along with my tears.
I send my prayers to you
wrapped with my swelling hopes.

In the pond of my humble heart,
I see a reflection of you
that pockets all the stars
I used to gaze upon.

Like bedtime stories,
the time has gone.
The child has become an island,
floating in the sea. Alone.

I won't yet stop dreaming of you
because I see in my garden of soul
a dandelion's yellow petals;
Undying desire, so small yet so dear.

[Note] This poem won the Editor's Choice Prize in 'The International Poetry Open
Contest, 2003' by the International Library of Poetry.(U.S.A.)

종이배

어제는
하얀 종이배
접었다 폈다

꽃 사월 먼 하늘가
어느 귀한 손님이 지나시기에
지빠귀 새들 아침부터 저리 부산스럽고
햇살은 은빛 가득히 찰랑이는가

흐르는 너와
흐르는 내가
앞서거니 뒤서거니 다다른
이승의 강가에서는

그리움 깊은 만큼 높이 나부끼고
살뜰히 못다 푸는 얽힌 인연에
목숨은 눈물겨운 비췻빛인데

오늘도
또 하얀 종이배
접었다 폈다 또 접었다.

[노트] 한국어 버전 "종이배"는 2011년 6월 '문예감성 푸른시인 덕유산 시화전' 참
여 작품으로 덕유산 무주구천동 숲 오솔길에 전시되었고, 영어 버전 "Paper Boat"
는 세계시낭송협회 시인들에 의해 다섯 언어로 번역, 캐나다, 미국, 한국, 중국,
헝가리, 프랑스, 호주에서 신문과 문예지에 소개되었음.

Paper Boat

Yesterday,
I folded and unfolded
A white paper boat.

Who is the noble—born high up there
Passing through the perfumed April air?
Why are robins busy singing at this early hour
And silvery sunrays ripple everywhere?

It's you
It's me
One followed by the other
Arrived on this side of mortal shore

Where yearnings flutter as high as they are deep,
Where Karma is yet to untangle from the tangled spool,
Where breath of life is like jade, precious and tearful.

Today again,
My white paper boat
I fold, unfold, and fold again.

[Note] The Korean version "종이배" was exhibited on the Mt. Deok—Yu in Muju, Korea, as a participatory work of 'The Blue Poets of The Literary Sensibility Exhibition', June 2011; And the English version "Paper Boat" was translated into five different languages by the WPRS poets, and published in the newspapers and magazines in five Countries.

빈센트
—밴 고흐의 그림 '귀에 붕대를 감은 자화상'에 바침

오늘도 추우신가, 사람아
한여름에도
성애 낀 심장이 시려서 어깨 떨던
외로운 사람아

멀쩡한 귀 하나 잘라내어
짝사랑 〈고갱〉에게 바치고서
가슴으로 철철 피 흘리며 히히 웃던
영혼 아픈 사람아

해바라기 샛노란 꽃잎으로
그대의 외로움을 가려주련?
사이프러스 짙푸른 그늘로
그대의 슬픔을 숨겨주련?

이 밤에도
하늘엔 그대가 그리다 버리고 간 별들이
상처 입은 물고기들처럼
바람 속에 파닥인다

오라, 나의 친구여
그대 외로움에 내 그리움 칭칭 엮고서
저 깊은 별들의 고향으로 날아오르자
아직도 아프신가, 오, 아름다운 사람아!

Vincent

– Dedicated to Gogh's 'Self–portrait with Bandaged Ear'.

Are you cold tonight, dear Vincent?
Even in the middle of summer days
shoulders trembled with frosted heart.
You, a lonely person!

Cut off one of your healthy ears
to offered it to your unrequited–love 'Paul Gauguin'
and vaguely laughed while bleeding within.
You, with an aching soul!

Would bright yellow sunflower petals
cover your loneliness?
Would dark green shade of cypress
hide your sadness?

Tonight too,
the stars you left scattered behind
flip–flopping in the wind
like some wounded fish in the sky.

Come, my friend.
Let's entwine your loneliness and my yearnings
and fly to the village of stars deep in the sky.
Are you still in pain, O beautiful Man!

별밤의 곡예사

누구의 그리움인가?
누구를 향한 그리움인가?
별 하나 꽁꽁…
나 하나 꽁꽁…*

늙은 분수처럼 잦아든 세월 뒤로
꽁꽁 숨어버린
나비 가슴
꽃 가슴
문둥이 같은 그리움은
어둠으로나 만나지나

영글다 만 가슴 들판을
밤바람 에돌다 가면
그대는
잉크 빛 하늘 속에 외로운 곡예사
외줄 끝에 매달려
별똥별로 오시는가
별 둘 꽁꽁…
나 둘 꽁꽁…

[노트] 별하나 꽁꽁… 별 둘 꽁꽁…, 한국 전래 아동 놀이의 말노래 (말리듬)이며,
밤하늘에 별을 세면서 부르던 말리듬이 발전한 것이다.

Acrobat in the Starry Night

Whose longing is it?
Whom is it longing for?
One star deep in the sky...
One star deep in my heart...

Time has gone dry like an old fountain
Hiding deep behind the Time;
The heart of a butterfly
The heart of a flower
The longing hearts, as sad as leper's,
Can see each other in the dark of the nights only!

When the night winds whirl away
From unripe field of the heart,
You are a lonesome acrobat
In the inky night sky
Coming as a shooting star
Dangling on a single rope!
Two stars deep in the sky...
Two stars deep in my heart...

[Note] One star deep in the sky... Two stars deep in the sky... is Korean
children's old chant when they count the stars in the night sky.

별바라기 연가(戀歌)

누가 부는 바람을 탓하랴
풍경(風磬)이야 여하튼 울어야 하는 것을

누가 우는 풍경을 탓하랴
세월이야 여하튼 흘러가야 하는 것을

누가 흐르는 세월을 탓하랴
꽃이야 여하튼 피고 져야 하는 것을

꽃 피고 꽃 지는 시간, 그 사이에서
너는 밤하늘에 빛나는 머나먼 별이고

열리고 닫히는 수많은 밤들, 그 갈피에서
나는 여하튼 너를 사랑하는 별바라기인 것을.

Stargazer Love Song

Who would blame the wind for blowing;
Wind—bells have to ring anyway.

Who would blame the wind—bells for ringing;
Time has to pass anyway.

Who would blame Time for passing;
Flowers have to bloom and fall anyway.

Bloom and fall, and in between,
You are a far—flung star, shining in the night sky.

Nights open, nights close, and in between,
I am a stargazer who loves you anyway.

계절(季節)과 시절(詩節)

이월

예쁘고 당찬 아가씨다
빙판의 계절을
감히 맨발로 건너와서는
동면의 심장 깊은 곳에
입맞춤하고
그대와 나의
영혼의 강물을 풀어놓는구나

해바라기꽃

우러르다
우러르다
길어진 목
인제는 도로 접어둘 수도 없어
그리운 심장일랑
다소곳이
하늘가 높다라니
해님 가까이에 걸어 두었네.

가을이 오네요

마로니에 가지 사이로
소슬바람 부네요
어스름 강둑에
낙엽이 구르네요
귀뚜라미 울음 위로
달이 뜨네요
친구 있는 먼 곳에
내 마음 서성거리네요
천천히, 아주 천천히
가을이 오고 있네요.

동안거

살얼음 깔고
흰 모포를 덮은 강이
낮게 낮게 흘러서
로터스랜드의 긴 삼동(三冬)을 간다
깊고
하얀
침묵

Of Seasons and Verses

February

Sweet, daring maiden is she
Braved
Across the frozen season
In bare feet
Kissed the hibernating hearts deep within
And let flow the rivers of the soul:
Yours and mine.

Sunflower

Looking up
Looking up
The elongated neck
Now grown too long to fold it back;
The yearning heart
Hung shyly
Up high in the sky
Near the sun.

Autumn is Coming

Through the Marronnier branches
A gentle breeze is passing
On the darkening riverbank
Fallen leaves are drifting
Over the crickets' ardent chirps
The full moon is rising
A friend is far, far away
And there, my heart is wandering
Slowly, oh, so slowly
Autumn is coming.

Winter Retreat

Over the thin ice
Under the white blanket
Low, low, flows the river
Passing the Lotusland's long winter;
Deep
White
Silence.

갈대의 서(書)

가을입니다
지성, 성숙, 그리움, 고독
그 투명한 언어들이
기도처럼 가슴에 둥지 트는 계절입니다
9월 한낮 살찐 태양에
어린 밤송이들 토실토실 살 오르고
별빛 흥건한 풀숲은
귀뚜리 모여 앉아 현(絃) 타는 소리
밤과 함께 감미롭게 깊어갑니다
나는 허허 비워 가난한 가슴
작은 바람에도 커다랗게 흔들리며
들판 가득 청잣빛 하늘을 머리에 이고
흰 스카프 목에 두르고 가을 들길에 섰습니다
깊을수록 손끝 시린, 그리움
그 소슬한 계절병을 앓으며
행여 어느 날 그대 이 길을 지나실까
사추(思秋)의 길목 하얗게 밝혀 놓고 기다립니다.

Letter of the Reeds

The autumn is here.
Intellect, maturity, longing, solitude,
The season of transparent words nestles
In the hearts like prayers.
In the September sun,
Young chestnuts are ripening.
Under the savannah of stars,
String-concertos the crickets playing-
Sweet and delightful as the night deepens.
And here I stand
Beneath the Celadon-blue firmament,
My heart helplessly sways in the wind
With a white scarf fluttering on my neck.
Yearning is a seasonal sickness;
The deeper the lonelier it gets.
Perhaps you will pass this road one day,
I light up the autumn roadside white, and wait.

화해

겨우내
보트는 강 이쪽에 벙어리처럼 놓여 있었다
때때로 비바람이 선체를 뒤흔들었고
어떤 때는 눈보라가 무섭게 발을 굴렀다
이따금 달빛 별빛 내려와서
꽁꽁 언 뱃전에 볼 비비기도 했지만
그런 밤엔 또 이김없이
소슬한 그리움이 지병처럼 도지기도 했지만
어느 때부턴가 봄이 왔다고
강 건너 나팔소리 왁자할 때도
서러워라!
가슴 깊은 곳 동상(凍傷)은 쉽사리 풀릴 줄을 몰랐다

천지에 눈 부신 햇살 찰랑대는 지금은 4월
강물엔 꽃 그림자 칸타빌레*로 흐르고
뱃전이 조심스레 몸 뒤척이며 속삭인다
벗겨진 페인트 다시 칠하고 돛대를 세우란다
개나리꽃 빛깔 깃발 하나 돛대 끝에 꽂고
높이 더 높이 하늘가에 휘날리란다
오오, 목 늘여 기다려온
그리운 4월이여!

Reconciliation

All through the winter season,
The boat sat mute on this side of the river.
Winds shook it hard sometimes
Blizzard stomped furiously other times.
From time to time, moonlight and starlight came down
And caressed the frozen boat.
On such nights, without exception,
Aching longing revived like a chronic disease.
When trumpets horned loudly across the river,
Heralding, spring has finally come.
But, how sad!
The frostbite lingered within for a while longer.

And now, finally, dazzling April is here.
Rivers flow cantabile* with flower petals afloat.
The boat, too, rocks and bends, and softly whispers—
It's time to repaint the boat and raise the mast.
Fasten a forsythia—yellow flag on top of it
And let it flutter high and higher still.
How I longed for you,
O Sweet April!

파랑 날개 물고기

한세월 전
여름 냇가에서 놓쳐버린 나의 노래는
심술쟁이 물고기가 집어삼키고
겨드랑이에 파아란 날개가 돋쳐
하늘 못 속으로 날아갔거늘

누이야
봄이 오는 들녘 끝을 바람으로 에돌다가
고개 꺾고 돌아와 눕는 오후엔
하늘 못에 장대 낚시 드리워 놓고
파랑 날개 물고기나 낚아볼까

자갈길 지나서 꽃길 지나서
곤두박질치며 안고 달려온
땀내 묻은 나의 삶의 바구니
이제는 덩그러니 한옆에 비켜 놓고

기다리다 기다리다 입질 없으면
그땐, 툭툭 털고 일어나
한 점 바람으로나 돌아갈까
누이야

[노트] "파랑 날개 물고기"는 나의 저서 제1호의 제목이자 그 책의 테마 시(詩)이기도 하다. ('시한울' 발행, 2004)

The Blue Winged Fish

Once upon a time
A mischievous fish in the summer stream
Gobbled up my unborn song of dream
And became the blue winged fish
Flew into the pond in the sky.

My Dear,
Like restless wind in the early spring
I wandered far and wide and returned wearily
Trying to catch the fish with the blue wings
I threw a fishing line deep in the sky.

In the journey of my life, I have passed
The graveled roads and the flowery paths
And now, I sit quietly on this solitary wayside
With the sweat stained basket at my side.

I will wait with no hurry
If I don't catch the blue winged fish at the end
Then, my dear,
I will get up and leave as light as the wind.

[Note] "The Blue Winged Fish" is the title of my first book as well as the theme of the book. (Published by 'Sihanul', 2004)

해무(海霧)

회색에 갇힌 둑길을 걷는다
짙은 안개는
하늘과 바다 사이를 지우고
바다와 나 사이를 지우고
섬으로 가는 모든 뱃길을 지운다
오래된 슬픔도 그 앞에 엎지르면
저 너른 안개의 옷자락에 다 지워질까
상처 입은 희망이라도 아주 가끔은
물빛 지느러미 하나 얻어 달고
저편 해안에 닿고 싶다
시력 잃은 배들은 부지런히 경적을 날리고
바다오리들은 침침한 하늘을 가며 끼룩거린다
누구를 저리도 간절히 부르는 걸까
누구에게 저렇게 열심히 대답하는 걸까
나도 마음의 목청 돋워 날려 보내면
뚜우… 뚜우…
그 소리 너의 섬에 닿을까?
그 소리 너의 귀에 닿을까?

Sea Fog

I walk on the dyke trapped in grey.

Thick fog relentlessly erases

Between sky and sea

Between sea and me

And all the waterways to the islands.

If I spill my aged sorrow here on the dike,

Will it be erased by the fog's wide sleeve too?

Though this hope is wounded,

I wish to borrow a pair of blue fins now and then

And swim to the other side of the shore.

Ships are diligently whistling in the sea.

Sea−ducks are busy quacking in the dim sky.

For whom are they calling desperately so?

To whom are they answering eagerly so?

If I blow my heart loudly enough,

Too- too-

Will the sound reach your island?

Will the sound reach your ears?

모래밭에 낙서들

저녁 식사 후, 심장이 근질거려서 게리포인트 바닷가에 나갔다. 썰물이 크게 진 뒤끝이라 모래밭은 꽤 넓게 노출되어 있었다. 하루에 한두 번씩 크게 제 가슴을 비우는 바다—

모래밭에는 오늘따라 사람들이 써놓은 낙서들이 꽤 많았다. 재미있는 그림들도 여럿 있고, 사람들의 이름도 헝겊 조각들처럼 여기저기 널려 있었다. "아무개는 아무개를 사랑한다"라는 내용의 글들이 그중 많았다. 누군가의 가슴에 꼭꼭 갇혔던 은밀한 감정 조각들이 저렇게 모래밭에 엎질러져 노출되고 있는가! 사람들은 모래밭에다 자신의 감정을 각혈하듯 토해 놓고서 한결 가벼워진 가슴으로 돌아갔을까?

나는 낙서들 가까이에 서서 한참 동안 소라껍질처럼 귀를 세우고 서 있었다. 내가 만약 더 열심히 귀를 모으고 들었다면, 혹시, 모래 위에 즐비하게 누운 그 낙서들의 귓속말을 들을 수 있었을까?

Scribbles on the Sand

After dinner, I went to the Garry Point Park Beach because my heart was itchy. The sand bed was quite widely exposed this evening. The sea that empties its heart twice a day—

There were lots of scribbles written by people on the sand: a few interesting drawings along with many names scattered like pieces of fabrics. Many of the texts were there that read, "Someone loves someone". The pieces of secret emotions that escaped someone's concealed hearts are laid there in the open air! Did people return home, feeling much lighter after they coughed out their secrets onto the sand just so?

I stood close to the scribbles with my ears pricked up like an empty conch shell for a while, and listened. If I listened more attentively, would I have been able to hear the whispers of the scribbles on the sand?

Part Four
제4부

ON THE ROAD AGAIN
다시 길 위에서

다시 길 위에서
−나의 뮤즈에게 2

사람들은 누구나
어머니의 자궁 밖으로 나오는 그 순간부터
간절한 영혼의 고향 하나 갖기 시작한다
그리고는 목 타는 그리움으로 그곳을 찾아 헤맨다
그리하여 어딘지 모르는 고향을 찾아 방황하는
인간의 정처 없는 나그넷길은 계속된다
우리가 찾아 헤매는 그곳은 과연 무엇이며 어디일까
우리 생명의 씨앗이 맨 처음 싹 튼
어머니의 자궁, 양수의 바다일까?
아니면, 어느 먼 전생에 두고 온 고향일까?

나이 들고 육체와 정신이 성장하면서
고향의 대상은 그때마다 바뀐다
아기 때는 어머니의 유방이 고향이었고
유아기에는 장난감이 고향이 되기도 했다
좀 더 나이 먹고 성년이 되면서,
어떤 이에게는 예술이나, 종교, 혹은 깊고 넓은 지식이
또 어떤 이에게는 돈, 명예, 혹은 권세가
그리고 거의 누구나 한두 번쯤은 이성에의 사랑이
간절한 마음의 고향이 되기도 한다.

그것이 예술이든, 지식, 혹은 종교이든
또는 돈, 명예, 혹은 권세이든
처음이듯 마지막이듯 한사리*치는 이성간 사랑일지라도
입술 부르트며 찾아가는 몸짓은 누구나 간절하다:
낙타가 오아시스를 찾아 불볕 속 사막을 건너듯
순례자가 자아의 신화*를 찾아 먼 순례의 길을 가듯
바다로 나갔던 연어가 모천(母川)을 찾아
제 몸 찢기며 강 상류로 역류하여 헤엄쳐 오르듯

시여!
내게도 발바닥 아프게 찾아가는 네가 있다
한 발짝 다가오기도 하고
한 발짝 물러서기도 하고
은빛 날갯짓 펄럭거리며 언제나 그쯤에서 손짓하는 너:
신기루의 성(城); 그리운 내 영혼의 고향!
그래서 오늘도 목마른 내 영혼은
물집 든 발 절름거리며 너를 찾고 있다
다시 길 위에서

On the Road Again
−To My Muse 2

Everyone, including you and me,
Starts to have a home of the yearning soul
From the moment came out of the mother's womb
And looking for it with a thirst in the heart.
Thus, the aimless journey of human beings continues
Looking for the home of the yearning soul.
What and where is it that we are looking for?
Could it be a sea of amniotic fluid;
A mother's womb where our life first sprouted?
Or, a hometown we left somewhere in a Previous Life?

As we grow physically and mentally,
Our home of the soul changes.
For babies, it was mother's breast.
In childhood, it was the toys.
As we get older and mature,
For some, art, religion, or deep and broad knowledge,
For others, it was money, fame, or power.
And almost everyone falls in love once or twice,
And then, love becomes the home of the soul.

Whether it is an art, knowledge, religion,

Or money, fame, power,

Or the Hansari[*]−like love between two opposite sexes,

The eagerness and thirst of the heart are the same;

Like camels crossing hot deserts looking for an oasis;

Like pilgrims on pilgrimage in search of personal legend[*];

Like salmon in the sea swim back with torn bodies

To upstream where they were hatched.

O Poetry!

I too have you whom I ardently look for with my sore feet.

One step closer sometimes

One step farther another times

Somewhere there, its silver wings beckon to me

A castle of mirage: dear home of my soul.

So, today too,

My thirsty soul is limping with blisters

On the road again

장밋빛 인생

퀘벡 구시가지 로열광장에
늙은 악사가 바이올린을 켜고 있다
그의 신들린 활대 끝에서
"장밋빛 인생"은 꿈결같이 피어나고
사랑의 물보라가 하늘가에 나부낀다
로렌스 강 푸른 바람이
악사의 눈가에서 하르르 떠다
이마 위 주름살 이랑마다 찰랑대는
가난한 악사의 넉넉한 행복
눈물겨워라!
국적 다른 언어들이 범람하는
혼잡한 광장의 한복판에서
거리의 악사가 묵언의 눈빛으로 말하는
*라 비 앙 로즈: 장밋빛 인생—
인생은
바이올린의 무아경 날갯짓 같은 거라고
삶의 군살 반쯤 보이며
분홍 장미꽃을 피워 올리는 거라고
혼신을 다하여.

−1996년 6월, 캐나다 퀘벡 구시가지 '로열광장'에서

[노트] '라 비 앙 로즈'는 프랑스의 대표적 여류 샹송가수 에디뜨 삐아프가 이브몽땅과 깊은 사랑에 빠졌을 때 직접 작사/작곡한 노래다.

La Vie en Rose

In Place Royale square of Quebec City,

An old musician is playing a violin.

On the tip of his obsessed bow

The "La vie en rose"** blossoms like a dream

And a spray of love flutters high in the air.

In the corner of the musician's eyes

Blue wind of the St. Lawrence River trembles.

In every line on his forehead

A poor musician's ample happiness−

How moving!

In the middle of the crowded Square

Where many different national languages overflow,

A street musician tells with his reticent eyes

*La vie en rose: A Rosy Life−

Life is

Like the ecstatic flapping of a violin's wing:

Showing a half of the hard side of living

While making pink roses blossom

With all your might.

−At the Royal Square in Quebec, Canada, June, 1996.

[Note] 'La Vie en Rose' is a song written/composed by Edith Piaf, a representative French female chanson singer, when she fell in love with Yves Montand.

박카스 신(神)과의 일탈

독일, 뮌헨의 10월 맥주 축제 마당엔
보이지 않는 환희의 에너지가 들썩거린다
둥지 떠나온 국적 다른 새들의
날갯짓이 현란하다
이런 이유로
저런 이유로
늑골 밑에 꼭꼭 숨어 있던 유리 날개들이
어둠으로부터 기어 나와서
하나둘, 박카스 신과 통쾌하게 손잡는다
이성과 감성 사이
현실과 꿈 사이
가로막혔던 가슴 속 육중한 장벽에
개선문만큼 커다란 문 하나 무상으로 활짝 열리고
문을 빠져나온
눈부신 유리 날개들이
거침없이 프리즘의 빛을 발하며
훨훨 날아오른다
해롱해롱, 술에 취하여
어찔어찔, 인생에 취하여.

-독일 뮌헨에서 해마다 10월에 열리는 맥주 축제,
"옥토버페스트"에서, 2006년 10월

Deviation with the God Bacchus

*October Fest in Munich, Germany,

Great energy unseen vibrates with joy.

Away from their nests

Tourist-birds' wings flap colourfully.

Because of this reason,

Because of that reason,

Glass-wings that were hidden under their ribs

Crawl out from the darkness

And happily, join hands one by one with Bacchus.

Between reason and emotion,

Between reality and dream,

A door as large as the Arc de Triomphe

Opens widely on the heavy wall in their mind.

Dazzling glass wings came out

Through the door without hesitation,

Radiating prismatic lights

And joyfully they soar up high.

Frolicking, drunk with alcohol.

Dizzy, drunk with life.

> – At the annual beer festival "Oktoberfest" in Munich,
> Germany, Oct., 2006.

춤추는 오로라

시간이 얼어붙은
검은 지평선
태초보다 캄캄한 어둠 속에서
하얀 빛기둥들이 춤추며 일어선다

눈부신 빛줄기들이 갈가리 찢겨 던져진다
하얀 커튼들이 머리 위에서 재주를 넘는다
연초록 빛줄기들은
파도 속 미역 줄기처럼 나부낀다

보라!
하늘 가득히 미쳐 날뛰는
빛의 몸부림
태양과 지구의 선정의 춤
영광의 날개를 단
용맹스러운 이누이트* 혼령들이 펼쳐내는
매스 게임—
매 스 게 임!

여기
부화하지 못한 지상의 무정란 가슴 하나
북극의 얼음 벌판에 서서
장엄한 북극광 아래 용트림을 한다

상흔의 비늘들 쩍쩍 갈라진 자리에
날개가 돋는다 매의 날개가 돋는다
아, 뜨거운 나의 욕망이여,
날고 싶다!

-2004년 12월, 캐나다, 노스웨스트 준주, 옐로나이프에서

[노트] 이 시의 영문편 Dancing Auroras는 "국제여성영화인협회(WIF), 2008 축제" 행사장에서 WPRS 대표시로 낭송했으며(Mar. '08); South Delta 미술협회와 WPRS, Pandora's Poets가 공동 주최한 "그림과 시의 만남, 2008" 전시장에 미술가 Donna D'Aquino 씨의 그림과 함께 전시되었다.

Dancing Auroras

Low on the horizon
Where time is frozen,
Earth is darker than the Beginning
And there arise arcs of light, dancing.

Bright Coronas are torn and thrown
Glowing Curtains somersault high above
Greenish streamers stretch and flutter
Like seaweeds in surging waves.

Look!
The sky has gone crazy−
Swirling lights and wild dances
Of the Sun and the Earth.
With trophy wings,
Mighty spirits of dead Inuit* are performing
A mass game−
M A S S G A M E!

Here, my unfertilized heart is watching
The magnificent auroras
Over the Arctic field, trying
To wriggle out of the thick dark shell.

I hear cracking sounds from my old pain
And a pair of hawk wings pushing out.
Oh, my burning desire
Of flying!

−Dec. 2004, Yellowknife, Northwest Territory, Canada

[Note] This poem, Dancing Aurora, was selected by the WPRS, and I recited at the event of "Woman's International Film Festival(WIF), Vncouver"(Mar. 21, 2008). Also, it was exhibited with a painting by artist Donna D'Aquino at "the South Delta Artist Guild and Pandora's & WPRS Poets Joint Exhibition, 2008".

원 달라, 프리즈

나는 하바나 성당 광장의 처녀 곡예사
뒤뚱뒤뚱 곡예 신발 신고
장미빛 예쁜 웃음 풀어 삶을 구걸해요
엄마는 갓난 동생 안고 마켓 광장 앞에 나앉고
아빠는 이른 새벽 카멜로* 타고
사탕수수 농장 불볕 속으로 일하러 갔어요
저기, cigar 파는 할머니도
바라데로 해변에서 소라 껍질 파는 할아버지도
핏줄기엔 포도주 빛 노래가 흐르는
내 가난한 이웃, 스페인의 후예들이어요
일 불만 주세요
카메라와 비디오 앞에서
꽃보다 예쁜 웃음 활짝 피워 드릴게요
나는 처녀 곡예사, 예쁜 관광 상품
어디서든 카메라 셔터 소리 들리면
이리 저리 달려가 손 벌리는 쿠바의 딸이어요
원 달라, 프리즈!

−2002년 12월, Cuba, Havana 성당 앞 광장에서

[노트] 카멜로(Camello): 몸체가 길고 낙타(Camel)처럼 양쪽 끝이 2층으로 된
Cuba 하바나 서민들을 위한 거대한 옴니버스이며, 한 번에 보통 300명 이상의 승
객이 탑승한다.

One Dollar, Please

I am a maiden acrobat at the Havana Cathedral Square,
Waddling on the acrobatic pole−shoes
With a pretty rosy smile, begging for a life
Mommy sits at the market place with my baby brother.
Daddy went to the sugar−cane plantation, early morning
Riding the Camello[*] to work in the scorching sun.
The old lady, selling cigars over there, and the old man,
selling conch shells on the Varadero beach, are of the
Spanish descents, my hungry neighbors
Whose wine colour songs still flow in their bloodstream
Please spare me a dollar;
I will bloom smiles prettier than flowers
In front of your cameras and videos.
A maiden acrobat I am: a pretty tourist product:
The daughter of Cuba who runs to and fro wherever
Camera shutter sound, and hold out a hand.
One dollar, please!

−At the Havana Cathedral Square, Cuba, Dec. 2002.

[Note] Camello: the huge omnibus for the common people in Havana, Cuba,
with two−tiered at both ends, that resembles a camel−usually jammed with 300
and more passengers at a time.

구원의 예수상* 앞에서

지극히 짧은 순간에
찰나보다도 더 짧은 바로 그 순간에
커다란 바람 한 점 일어 안개 베일 걷히고
나는 드디어 당신을 볼 수 있었습니다.

리우데자네이루 코르코바도 정상에서
해협 건너 슈거로프의 청정한 정수리와
발아래 '케리오카'들의 삶을
구석구석 굽어보시는 당신은
구원과 믿음의 상징일 뿐만 아니라
하나의 크고 완벽한 예술의 극치였습니다.

30m 키에 635톤의 거대한 형상
크나크신 님
그윽하고 거룩한 모습이여!

나의 존재는 당신 앞에서 일순간에 사라지는 듯하고
마치 우주가 처음 열리던 그 날이거나
빛이 탄생하던 그 환희의 순간을
나, 직접 목격하는 듯했습니다.
가슴에 모은 두 손이 후들후들 떨리고
심장이 우릉우릉 천둥 치더이다.

　　　　　　　-브라질, 리우데자네이루, 코르코바도 山 정상에서, 2009년 11월

In Front of Christ the Redeemer[*]

In a very short moment,
Even shorter than a blink of an eye,
A strong wind blew and the veil of the fog lifted;
Thus, I was able to see you at last.

From the top of 'Corcovado' in Rio de Janeiro,
Looking down the clean crown of 'Sugar—Loaf'
Across the strait and the lives of Cariocas
In every nook and corner;
Not only a symbol of faith and salvation, but also,
A big and perfect beautiful artwork was you.

30m tall and 635t of massive body;
So profound and holy figure
So large and great looking!

My existence seemed to disappear in front of you.
I felt as if I were witnessing, either
The moment the Universe was first formed, or
The wondrous moment when the Light was born.
My hands on my chest trembled with awe.
My heart boomed loudly like thunder too.

—On top of Corcovado Mountain in Rio de Janeiro, Brazil, Nov. '09.

135

비밀 속의 마추픽추

먼먼 나라 잉카의 산골짝
수많은 돌층계를 오르내렸습니다
인디오의 거대한 콘도르는 보이지도 않고
잉카 왕국 마지막 추장의 슬픈 흐느낌만
비와 바람의 통곡 사이에서
얼핏 설핏 어렴풋이 들은 것 같습니다

황금 잉카 제국은 어디로 갔을까요?
안데스산맥의 콘도르들은 혹시 알까요?

인디오 석공들의 망치 소리도
잉카 제국의 아침을 열던 귀족들의 힘찬 북소리도
태양 처녀들의 실 잣는 물레 소리도
이제는 모두 세월의 바다에 방생되고
까마득한 절벽 아래로
우루밤바 강물은 무심한 듯 유유한데
마추픽추 그림자를 가슴에 품고
잉카 제국의 비밀을 늑골 깊이 감춘 채
비와 구름과 햇빛의 자리바꿈만
저네들끼리 분주하더이다.

－2009, 11월, 페루 '마추픽추' 잉카 공중도시에서

Machu Picchu in Its Secret

I went up and down the stone stairs
In the Inca valley of the faraway country.
I have not heard nor seen the majestic eagles,
But instead, I think I faintly heard sorrowful moan
Of the last chief of the Golden Inca Empire
In between the lamenting rain and wind.

Where has the Golden Inca Empire gone?
Perhaps the condors of the Andes Mountains know?

The hammering of the Indio masons,
The powerful drumming of the Inca nobles,
That used to open the Inca Empire mornings,
And the sound of spinning wheel of the Sun Maidens,
All have been released into the Ocean of Time.
Far down at the deep dark cliff,
The heedless Urubamba River meanders idly
Embracing the shadow of Machu Picchu in its bosom;
Hiding the secret of Inca Empire deep under its ribs;
Only the rain, clouds, and sunlight were busy
Alternating places with each other.

—At Machu Picchu, Inca Citadel in Peru, Nov. 2009.

이구아수 폭포의 참모습

이구아수 폭포의 참모습을 만나려거든
그대여,
하늘에 구멍 커다랗게 뚫리고
소낙비 억수로 쏟아지는 날을 택해서 가소

소낙비 퍼붓던 그 한낮
풀잎처럼 작고 가냘픈
동양계 여자와
세계 최대 폭포 이구아수는 그렇게 만났느니

하늘과 땅이 물 하나로 통하고
천국과 연옥이 물 하나로 뒤엉겨져
물 물 물…
천지가 온통 물의 광란이더이다

은빛 물 커튼들과 영롱한 무지개의
환상적인 기념사진들은 못 찍어도
이구아수 폭포의 참모습을 보기 원하거든
그대여, 소낙비 억수로 퍼붓는 날을 택해서 가소

그리하여 우리가 이 세상에 와서 익힌
때 묻은 언어들은 한순간에 씻겨져 내리고
몇 겹 전생의 때도
모두 씻겨져 떠내려가고

아아, 지구가 처음으로 숨통 트던 그 순간의 소리
그대는 들으리니
그리고 저 위대한 대자연 앞에
경건하게 무릎 꿇는 그대 자신을
그대는 보려니!

-2009년 11월, 브라질, 이구아수 폭포에서

The True Nature of Iguazu Falls

If you want to see the true nature of Iguazu falls,
Dears,
Choose a torrential rainy day
With a big hole break open in the sky.

One midday, in the pouring rain,
An Asian−born woman,
Small and meek as a blade of grass,
Met Iguazu the world's largest waterfalls.

Sky and earth are one, mingled with water.
Heaven and hell are one, intertwined with water.
Water, water, water⋯
It was a madness of water between heaven and earth.

Even though we cannot take commemorative photos
With silver water−curtains and fantastic rainbows,
If you want to see the true naked Iguazu falls,
Then my dears, choose a day of very heavy rain.

And so, the tainted languages we learn in This world
Will be instantly washed away, and
Stains from many Previous lives
Will also be cleansed and washed away.

You will then hear the sound
Of the Earth took her first breath;
And see yourself kneeling down reverently
Before Great Mother Nature!

—At Iguazu Falls, Brazil, November, 2009

낙타의 눈

낙타의 눈을 본 적 있네. 나일강 언저리 작은 오아시스 마을에서
였네. 아라비아사막의 자투리 모래땅을 낙타는 천천히 걷고 있었
네. 열 살쯤 된 남루한 소년을 등에 태우고 옆구리엔 커다란 가
죽 물주머니를 느슨하게 매달고 고개를 반쯤 숙인 채 그는 충직
한 노비처럼 걸어오고 있었네. 어느 한순간, 그와 나의 눈이 마주
쳤고 바로 그 순간, 호기심 많은 나의 마음이 나도 모르는 사이에
겹겹 긴 속눈썹으로 가려진 그의 눈 속 그 너머 깊은 곳으로 훌쩍
뛰어들었네.

거기 늙은 낙타의 눈 속에서 나는 들었네. 작열하는 태양에 달궈
진 모래 언덕을 넘던 지친 캐러밴들의 무거운 발소리와 별빛 푸
른 밤이면 캐러밴의 무리 따라 사막을 건너던 선조 낙타들의 긴
목에서 쩔렁쩔렁 울던 방울 소리를— 그리고 또 들었네. 바다가
사막으로 걸어 들어가기 수백만 년 전에 그곳에서 철썩이던 파도
자락들이 아직도 늙은 낙타의 젖은 눈 안에서 메아리치는 소리와
기자 피라미드 암석에 박힌 화석들처럼 시간의 가슴에 오롯이 새
겨진, 스핑크스보다 훨씬 늙은 사막의 곰삭은 역사 이야기를—

그렇다네! 나는 낙타의 젖은 눈을 본 적 있네: 하도 깊고, 어둡고,
비밀스러워서 오히려 슬퍼 보이던 눈을.

—2011년 1월, 이집트 나일강 강가 어느 오아시스 마을에서

Camel's Eye

I've seen a camel's eye. It was in a small oasis village by the Nile River. He was walking slowly in the sand field at the edge of the Arabian Desert, with his head half lowered like a loyal old servant, carrying a shabby boy of about ten—year—old on his back and a large leather water—bag loosely at his side. At one moment, his and my eyes met. At that very moment, without any intention, my inquisitive mind jumped into his eyes behind the long double—layered eyelashes.

There in the camel's eyes, I heard; weary caravans' heavy footsteps crossing the heated sand dunes in the scorching sun, and the sound of the bells on the long necks of the ancestor camels following caravans on blue starry nights— And also, I heard; the sound of splashing waves many millions of years before the sea had walked into the desert, that still echoes in the old camel's wet eyes, and the history of the desert—much older than the Sphinx— engraved in the bosom of time like the fossils in the Giza pyramids' rock.

That's right! I've seen a camel's wet eyes: so deep, dark and secretive, somehow, they looked sad.

—At an oasis village by the Nile River, Egypt. Jan. 2011.

임진각 공원*

남쪽, 북쪽, 민주주의, 공산주의—
이데올로기와 정치 체제의 언어들이
임진각 리조트 벽면에
독거미들처럼 기어 다닌다.
자유를 추구하다 부러진 날개들이
수많은 기념비와 흑백 사진 속에서
철철 피 흘리며
전 세계 관광객들을 불러모은다.

슬픔, 고통, 필사의 비명
탈출, 난민, 이산가족—
오, 상처받은 언어들이여!
오, 쓰러져간 영웅들이여!
부디 편히 쉬십시오
그대 젊고 용맹스럽던 혼령들이여,
당신들의 마지막 절규, 온 세상이 듣고 있습니다.
당신들이 흘린 피, 절대로 잊히지 않을 것입니다.

—2017년 10월, 모국 방문 때 경기도 파주시, 임진각에서

Imjingak Park[*]

South, North, Democracy, Communism—
The words of ideology and political systems—
Crawl like poisonous spiders
On the walls of [*]Imjingak Park.
Behind every monument and photo frames,
Broken wings of the freedom pursuers
Still bleeding,
Calling tourists from around the world.

Griefs, pains, desperate scream
Escapes, refugees, dispersed families
Oh, the wounded words!
Oh, the fallen heroes!
Please rest in peace,
You, young and valiant souls.
Your last scream; The whole world is listening.
The blood you shed; Will never be forgotten!

— At Imjingak Park in Paju, Kyung—Gi Province, while visiting South Korea,
my home—country. Oct. 2017.

찻집 '고독'

너는 잿빛 안개비 속에 하얀 부표처럼 떠 있었다

바다엔 잔뜩 노한 파도들이 줄줄이 달려와서 시멘트 방파제에 부
딪혀 부서지는데, 갈매기들의 껄껄대는 소리가 있어야 할 자리엔
성난 바다의 고함만 점령군처럼 도도했다
나의 차는 해안선을 끼고 달리고 있었다
좁디좁은 공간엔 길 떠난 이가 뒤통수에 달고 다니는 향수와 목젖
아픈 그리움이 곰팡이처럼 층층이 돋아있었다 갓 구워낸 빵 냄새,
향긋한 녹차 향기, 따뜻한 난롯가의 두런대는 목소리—
아아, 마디마디 저며오던 외로움이여!
적실 수 없는 영혼의 간절한 목마름이여!
네가 파도 끝에 둥둥 떠서 하얀 가슴을 벌려준 건 바로 그때였다
바다의 분노와는 아랑곳없다는 표정으로 너는 고향처럼 거기서
날 기다리고 있었다 톱밥이 훨훨 타고 있는 너의 난롯가에 추위
타는 나의 영혼을 낙엽처럼 벗어 놓으면 넉넉한 미소로 다 받아
줄 것만 같던 너—
나는 항구에 밀려온 난파선처럼 황황히 닻을 내리고 너의 가슴
안으로 빨려들었다

그해 늦가을 날,
안개비 내리는 주문진 바닷가의 하얀 찻집
너, '고독' 안으로!

—2013년 10월, 강릉 주문진 바닷가의 찻집 '고독'에서

146

The Teahouse 'SOLITUDE'

You were floating like a white buoy in the grey misty rain.

Angry waves surged onto the shore in rows at the sea, crashing against the cement breakwater incessantly. The sound of the seagulls was replaced with the lordly roars of the angry Sea.

My car was running alongside the coastline. In the tiny space of the car, nostalgia and longing grew thick in layers like moss: the smell of freshly baked breads, the aroma of sweet jasmine tea, the murmur of familiar voices around a warm fireside.

Ah, the unbearable loneliness!

The thirst of an unquenchable soul!

It was then, I saw your white chest on the end of waves. As if you were not aware of the raging sea, you stood aloof there waiting for me like an old hometown. If I shook off my cold soul like fallen leaves beside your sawdust burning stove, you would have accepted my soul with a broad smile.

I, like a shipwreck, hurriedly dropped my anchor and rushed into you.

On that late autumn day,

The white teahouse on Jumunjin Beach in the misty rain,

You, SOLITUDE!

-At the Teahouse SOLITUDE on Jumunjin Beach, Gangneung, South Korea. Oct. 2013.

147

Part Five
제5부

FRAGRANCE OF
HUMAN−FLOWER
인간 꽃 향기

인간 꽃 향기

꽃은 식물의 얼굴
향기는 식물의 미소여라
사람의 얼굴은 인간 꽃
사람의 미소는 인간 꽃의 향기여라

경이로워라!
모든 향기는 독특하고 아름답구나
인간 꽃 향기는
그 중에도 가장 아름답구나

사랑하는 이여,
만약 그대와 나의 향기가 함께 어우러져
우리의 삶을 더욱 밝고 기분 좋게 한다면
참으로 멋진 일이 아니겠는가

Fragrance of Human-Flower

Flowers are the faces of the plants;
Fragrances are the smile of the plants.
A human face is a human—flower;
Human smile is the fragrance of a human—flower.

How marvelous!
All fragrances are unique and beautiful;
Fragrance of human—flower is
Most beautiful of them all.

My dear,
If the fragrance of yours and mine put together
Makes our life bright and delightful,
Wouldn't it be truly wonderful?

오수(午睡)
−빈센트 반 고흐의 그림 〈오수〉에 바침

한가을 살찐 색깔들이
우르르 떼 지어 몰려와 눕는다
햇살 촘촘한 이 한낮엔
들숨 날숨 온통 황금빛이구나
하늘의 뜻을 받들고
땅의 관용을 믿는 지순한 당신
고된 노동 끝에
행복한 오수에 드는구나
휴식은
하늘의 축복
정직한 땀방울 위에 내리는
숭고한 트로피
당신의 소박한 꿈 날개가
조용조용 청잣빛 하늘을 두드리나니
그 꿈길 부디 종교처럼 깊고
비둘기 눈빛처럼 고요하기를!

The Siesta
-Dedicated to "The Siesta" by Vincent Van Gogh-

The rich colours of the autumn day

Flood in groups and lie down.

In this sunny midday

Inhalation and exhalation, all golden.

Respecting the Will of the heavens

Believing the tolerance of earth

You are now taking a happy midday nap

After the laborious toil.

Resting is

A blessed reward

A divine trophy

Upon the honest sweat.

The wings of your humble dream

Softly tap the ceiling of the azure dome.

May the path of your sleep as deep as religion

And as peaceful as the eyes of doves!

신혼부부들에게
–나의 아들들과 며느리들에게

보이지 않는 인연의 강물 따라
수천 년을 흘러 흘러
이승의 강가에서 다가선 두 개의 섬
한 쌍의 부부여라. 너희는!

인생이란
연습도 각본도 없는 단 한 번뿐인 공연
때로는 열심히 물구나무서는 곡예사로
때로는 포기를 모르는 칠전팔기 오뚝이로
미래의 행복을 추구하는 것이니

삶의 소중한 순간들은
웃음으로 눈물로 함께 보듬고
어둡고 서늘한 곳에서 좋은 술을 익히듯
고통과 분노는 사랑으로 승화시키며

맛깔스러운 삶 하나 함께 엮기 위하여
한평생 다 하도록 손잡고 달려야 하니라
잘 신고 잘 닳아 편안한 한 켤레 구두같이 될지니
반드시 그러할지니. 너희는!

To the Newlyweds

−For my sons and daughters−in−law

After meandering many thousand years
Along the invisible River of Destiny,
Two Islands meet on the shore of This World,
Become one loving couple. So are You!

Life is
One−time−only show; no rehearsal nor script.
Pursuing a happy future
As an acrobat cartwheeling mightily;
As a tumbling−doll that knows no surrender.

With laughter and with tears,
Embrace the precious moments together;
Try to sublimate pains and angers with love
As brewing a good wine in the dark and cool shade.

In order to weave one beautiful life together,
Run hand−in−hand all the way to the end,
Comfortable and content like a pair of shoes well−worn.
You will. You sure will!

귀여운 마법사
−손주 D에게 1

아가야,
우리 가족에 기쁨과 사랑을 가져다주는
너는 참으로 놀라운 마법사다

네 예쁜 고사리손을 꼭 잡고 있으면
나이 든 내 뼈마디의 아픔과 통증이
마술지팡이처럼 말끔히 사라지는 걸 보면

너의 흑진주 두 눈을 들여다보고 있으면
내 안에 드리웠던 근심 걱정의 그림자가
새벽하늘처럼 환하게 걷히는 걸 보면

너의 천진난만한 옹알이를 듣고 있으면
북극해처럼 꽁꽁 얼었던 마음도
봄눈처럼 스르르 녹는 걸 보면

태어난 지 이제 겨우 두 달 된 너
주위엔 평화와 기쁨의 아우라가 춤을 춘다
예쁜 아가야,
너는 정녕 경이로운 마법사구나!

Sweet Wizard
−To My Grandson D. 1

Little darling, D.
Bringing love and light into our family
You are such an amazing wizard.

When I hold your cute little hands
Pains and aches instantly disappear from
My aged bones as if touched by a magic wand.

When I behold your pearly dark eyes
Shadow of anxieties and worries lift up
As clear as the dawning sky.

When one listens to your innocent babbling,
Any heart, frozen like the North Pole at times,
Will slowly melt like snow in the spring sun.

You are but two−moons−old now, yet
Aura of peace and joy dances around you
Sweet D,
A truly marvelous wizard, you are!

간절한 기도
-손주 D에게 2

축구공 따라 뛰어다니며 크는
너를 지켜보면서
내 가슴은 따뜻하게 기도로 차오른다.

너의 인생 여로엔
이마에 뜨거운 땀 흘리는 날 종종 있겠지만
네 행복한 미래를 위해 흘리는 숭고한 땀이기를—
눈물 흘리는 날도 더러 있겠지만
네 영광의 순간에 흘리는 환희의 눈물이기를—

한국계 캐나디안 제1세대인
네 할아버지와 할머니의 소원은 오직 하나
여기 이민의 땅에서 너희가
사회의 기둥으로 반듯하고 튼튼하게 자라도록
좋은 밑거름이 되어 주는 것이니

비록 우리가 걸어온 지난 50년은
동방의 삶 서방 세계에 접목하는
땀투성이 도전의 세월이었지만
개척자의 고단한 삶은 인제 그만
네 할아버지와 나에게서 끝날 것이다.

활짝 펼쳐진 밝은 미래는 너와 네 자손의 몫
크고 중요한 일들이 너를 기다리고 있느니
너의 생각은 항상 숭고할 것이며
열심히 가꾸고 풍성히 거두며
소중하게 누리고 두루 나누며
그리하여 타인에게 존경받는 인물이 되어
자자손손 길이길이 번영하여라.

오늘도, 트랜스포머 장난감을 가지고
재밌게 노는 너를 바라보면서
지금 네가 가지고 노는 작은 장난감들이
네 미래의 큰 장난감 "*세계*"가 되도록 해주십사고
네 할머니의 가슴이 이렇게 간절한 기도로 차오름을!
사랑하는 손주야, 너는 아느냐?

The Earnest Prayers
−To My Grandson D. 2

Watching you grow, while
You run around following the soccer balls
My heart wells up warmly with earnest prayers.

During the journey of your life
There will be days you sweat hot on your forehead,
Let them be sublime sweat for your happy future.
There will be tears, too, from your eyes at times,
Let them be tears of joy upon your glorious moments.

Your grandfather and I,
The first−generation of Korean−Canadian,
Have one wish: becoming good fertilizer for you
To grow proper and strong as pillar of the society
Here in this land of immigration.

Though our roads for the past 50 years
Have been sweaty with full of challenges
Grafting the Eastern life into the Western,
But the settlers' hard life will end right here with us
Your grandfather and me.

The bright future widely spread out is all yours

And there are big and important duties waiting for you.

So, please be high-minded always

Cultivate hard and harvest bountifully,

Cherish and share with others,

Thus, become a person respected by many people

And prosper for many generations down the road.

Again today, while watching you having fun

With the Transformers toys,

Your grandmother's heart fills up with earnest prayers;

Please, let the little toys you play with now

Become the big toy "*The World*" of the future

My dear grandson, do you know?

소중한 것들

정가표가 없었네
흥정이 필요 없었네
물처럼 공기처럼
늘 그렇게 곁에 있었네−
검은 머리 부모님들
치맛자락에 매달리던 어린것들
꽃다운 나의 젊은 날

왜 진작에 몰랐을까
가장 귀한 것들에는
가격표가 없다는 것을
늘 그 자리에 있을 것 같던 나의 젊음도
문득 뒤돌아보면
이미 돌아오지 않는 세월의 강을 건너
가버리고 없는데

왜 좀 더 일찍이 몰랐을까
그들이 내 곁에서 영원히 떠나가고 말면
이토록 사무치게 그리울 줄을!

The Precious Things

No price tags were posted
No bargains were needed
Like air, like water
They were there always easily at hand:
My parents in their black hair
My little rascals around my apron
My flowery days of yesteryear.

Why hadn't I known it sooner?
The most precious things
Have no price tags at all.
By the time I realized it
Time had flown away
And my prime years, too, long gone
Across the River of no return.

Why hadn't I known it much sooner?
After they left me forever
I would miss them so dearly!

어머니의 바다

어머니, 그곳이 큰 바다였음을
저는 전혀 기억하지 못해요
그 양수의 바다에 한 톨 생명으로 헤엄쳐 다닐 때
그 따뜻함, 평화로움 그리고 그 완벽한 편안함—

그런데 어머니,
죄송스럽게도 저는 그 모든 걸 다 잊었어요
당신의 바다에서 소리치며 뛰쳐나오던 순간
제 배꼽에서 잘려져 나간 물빛 푸른 지느러미를
아주 까맣게 잊었듯이

세상에 나와서 세상 물 들어가는 동안
저 또한 당신이 주신 "여자"라는 빛나는 이름으로
사랑을 배우고
생명을 잉태하고
모정을 바치고
이제 헐거워진 어깨뼈 위로
치자 빛 노을이 내려요

알게 혹은 모르게
참 멀리도 걸어와 버린 이승의 나들잇길에
다시 한번 찬란한 봄이 열리고
다시 한번 라일락 축제 하늘가에 그윽한데

그런데 저는 왜 뜬금없이 눈물이 나나요, 어머니?
그 따뜻하고 아늑한 어머니의 방이
오늘은 이토록 그리운가요
기억에도 없는 당신의 바다가.

Mother's Ocean

Dear Mother, I cannot remember
That it was a big Ocean.
When I swam freely as a Seed of Life there,
The warmth, peace and perfect comfort.

But, Mother,
I am sorry, I completely forgot,
As I forgot the blue fin cord removed
From my belly soon after I jumped out
Of your Ocean into This World.

While going through this Land of Living,
I, too, in the radiant name "woman" you gave me,
Learned to love
Became a mother
Offered maternal affection.
And now, evening-glow is descending
Upon my frail shoulders.

Knowingly, and unknowingly, I've walked so far
On the trail of my outing in This World.
Once again, the splendid spring has opened;
Once again, the fragrant lilac festival is in the air.

But then, why suddenly am I tearful, dear Mother?

I miss your ocean so much today—

The warm and cozy maternal room

That I don't even remember.

애모(哀慕)

학처럼 고고(孤高)하게
연꽃처럼 지순(至純)하게
어진 선비처럼 의연(毅然)하게
이승 길 한 자락 조용히 밝히시며

천금보다 귀한 삶의 교훈
육 남매의 혈맥 깊이
유산(遺産)으로 심어주시고

이제는
고향 산(山)
솔바람 덮고 쉬시네.

[노트] 나의 친정아버님 묘비에 새겨진 시.

Deeply Missed

Aloft and refined like a white crane
Clean and pure like a lotus flower
Gentle yet resolute like a virtuous scholar
Quietly illuminating your path in This World.

A life—lesson more precious than thousand gold
Planted deep as a legacy
Into your six children's blood vessels.

Now, you are peacefully resting
On the hometown mountain side
Covered with the gentle breeze.

[Note] The epitaph on my father's gravestone.

짧은 재회

차표를 끊는다
유년으로 가는 먼 추억 행
맨발의 내 심장이
세월의 뒤안길로 앞서 달려간다.

고속도로, 고층 아파트들 들어서기 전
보리밭 둑길 지나 실개천 건너
조붓한 골목길 끝닿은 거기
그리운 내 유년의 추억이 묻힌 곳
파란 대문 집 문 앞에서
중년의 웃음 환히 웃고 계시는 아버지를 만난다.

"아버지,
거기 이승 밖 세월이 불편치 않으세요?"
"아니다, 애야,
고혈압, 신부전증 다 벗고
인간 세상 희로애락 모두 내려놓고
바람에 헹군 영혼 새벽같이 맑으니라."

새삼 복받쳐 오르는 그리움
아버지의 두 손을 덥석 잡으려다 보니
아뿔싸!
딸보다 젊은 아버지는 세상 저쪽에
아버지보다 늙은 딸은 세상 이쪽에
두 장승처럼
아득히 바라보며 마주 서 있다.

끝 간 데 없는 창공에
하얀 양떼구름 몇 무리 한가로이 어슬렁거린다.

A Brief Reunion with My Father

I buy a ticket;
A long—distance ticket to my childhood years.
My barefoot heart runs ahead of me
To the time past far yonder:

Before the highway and the high—rises were built
Across the creek by the barley field
At the end of the small alley
In front of the blue gate house
Where my sweet childhood memories are buried
I meet my middle—aged father smiling broadly.

  "Dear father,
  Aren't you uncomfortable there in the World Beyond?"
  "Not at all, my dear daughter.
  No high blood—pressure, no renal diseases,
  Free from human emotions: joy, anger, sorrow, pleasure,
  My soul, washed by the wind, is as fresh as the dawn."

With sudden gush of a longing,

I try to grab my father's hands eagerly.

But alas!

My father, younger than me, is there in the world beyond,

And I, older than my father, am here in this world,

Looking at each other from afar,

Like two wooden statues.

And there in the bottomless Celadon firmament,

Herds of white clouds leisurely roam about.

무채색(無彩色)

단 한 번도
제 색깔을 고집한 적 없다
물의 아름다운 본질을 닮아
우주의 모든 색깔을
마다치 않고 제 안에 끌어안을 뿐
그러나 단 한 시도
저 자신의 색을 잃은 적 없다
공기처럼
바람처럼
거울의 속 살처럼
있는 듯 없고 없는 듯 있는 무채색의 색

*색즉시공, 공즉시색**

흐르는 강물에 손을 씻듯
세상에 대한 온갖 감정의 색깔과
자기 애착의 색깔을 씻어버리고
숭고한 그 마음 하나로
삼라만상 모든 색의 본질에 닿아
싸잡아 너그러이 제 품에 보듬을 뿐.

Achromatic Colour

Not even once

Has it insisted on its own colour;

It embraces all colours of the universe

With no resistance

Like the intrinsic beauty of water.

And yet, not even for one moment

Has it lost its own colour;

Like air

Like wind

Like the core of a mirror−

The colour within achromatic colour.

Form is Emptiness; Emptiness is Form[*]

Like washing hands in a flowing river,

Wash away the colour of all emotions for the world

And the colour of attachment to one's own self;

The sublime heart resonates

With the essence of every colour in every form

And cradles them all in its benevolent arms.

단단한 선(線)들
─입동일(立冬日) 아침에

지난가을의 마지막 날에 잠이 들고
이 겨울의 첫날에 잠이 깼다
보이지도 만져지지도 않는
시간의 경계들이
보이지도 만져지지도 않는
세월의 도화지 위에
단단한 선(線) 한 개 더해 놓고
또 하나의 계절을 데리고 갔구나
얼마나 많은 춘하추동이 그렇게 쏜 살처럼
나를 스쳐 갔는가?

말도 안 돼!
말도 안 돼!
허공에 대고 손사래 쳐보지만
내 머리 위에 죽치고 앉은 서리꽃들이
말없음표 희끗희끗 고개를 주억거린다
원하던 원치 않던
시간은 여전히 내 위로 흘러갈 터이고
원하던 원치 않던
또 다른 단단한 선들이
내 인생의 화폭에 더해질 게 아니냐며

겨울을 건너가는 꽃씨처럼 살라 한다
우주적 생명의 리듬에 기대어
자는 듯, 그러나 깨어서
매 순간 가득하게 살라 한다.
매 순간 가득하게 살라 한다.

The Solid Lines

—In the Morning of First Winter Day

Fell asleep on the last day of last fall,

Woke up the first day of this winter.

Though invisible and untouchable,

The borderline of every hour

added one more solid line

On the canvas of time

That is also invisible and untouchable,

And took away one season with it

How many seasons flew by me

Just like an arrow?

No way!

No way!

I wave hands in the air in denial.

But the frost—flowers, perched on my head,

Nod heads with white silent words, saying:

Whether I want it or not

Time will continue to flow over me.

Whether I want it or not

Another solid line will be drawn

On the canvas of my life anyway.

Live like a flower seed crossing winter:

Lean on the Cosmic rhythm of Life,

As if sleeping yet awake,

And live every moment in its fullness.

And live every moment in its fullness.

인간의 자식들 2

삶과 꿈의 갈피에는
보이지 않는 오솔길이 있다
먼 광야 휘돌아온 바람이 그것을 알고
거대한 밤하늘 속 별들도 그걸 말해준다
눈물과 웃음의 사이에도 언제나
희망의 다리 하나쯤 숨어 있다
겨울을 건너온 봄꽃들에서
큰비 지난 뒤 무지개에서 그걸 볼 수 있다
생명 있는 모든 것은
아름다운 *'자아의 신화' 하나씩 간직하고 있다
사막의 꽃들이 그것을 보여주고
물길 거슬러 가 산란하는 연어들도 그걸 보여준다
다만, 인간의 자식으로 태어난
그대와 나
그와 그녀만이
이 아름다운 진리를 때때로 잊을 뿐

한 발짝 물러서서 보니, 보인다 조금씩
인생길 이만큼 걸어와 보니, 알겠다 조금은

Children of Human Womb 2

There are secret pathways

Hidden between living and dreaming;

The wind that came through a plain knows it so

Circling stars in the dark immensity tell us too.

There is a bridge of hope

Hidden between tears and laughter;

See it for yourself in the spring flowers

And rainbows after big rain storms.

Every living being holds

Its beauty of *Personal Legend;

Desert flowers show us

So do the spawning salmon upstream.

It's only you and me

And he and she

The children of human wombs

Oblivious about the beautiful truth at times.

Taking a step back and look; I could see it little by little.

Walking this far in life journey; I came to know it a little.

어머니 가시던 날

떠나셨다.
간병인 손에 정결히 몸 씻으신 뒤
곁에 있는 아들과 며느리조차 알세라 모를세라
고요히, 편안히 주무시듯 가셨단다
오로지 베풂의 생애였던 구십오 년 당신 평생에
헤아릴 수 없는 깊은 모정(母情)
자손들 위에 아낌없이 베풀어주시고
가을 하늘처럼 넉넉한 온정도
친척과 이웃에게 골고루 나눠주시고
스물다섯 해 전에 이승을 떠나신 사랑하는 지아비 곁으로-
우리 육 남매의 그리운 아버님 곁으로-
새처럼 나비처럼 훨훨
우리 어머니 조용히 날아가시더란다.
"가는 바람은 나뭇잎 흔들고
맑은 달빛은 수구에 고였다…"
생전에 즐겨 읊으시던 어머니의 18번 낭송 시(詩)도
이제는 꽃잎처럼 고이 접혀 주인 따라 영원으로 날아갔는데
어쩌나!
어머니의 그 낭송 소리 다시 듣고 싶을 때면
나 정말로 어찌하나?

[노트] 친정어머니, 2022년 1월 11일 낮 1시에 편안히 영면에 드시다.

The Day Mother Passed Away

She left.
After bathe given by her caregiver
As if didn't want to bother anyone,
Even her son and daughter−in−law close by her side,
Peaceful and comfortable, she left in her sleep: they say.
Her ninety−five−years had been a life of a giving;
Unfathomable was her genuine maternal love
Dedicated upon her children.
Generous like autumn sky was her heart
Toward her relatives and neighbours.
To meet her loving husband−our dear late Father
Who had left this world twenty−five years ago,
Mother gently fluttered away
Like a bird, like a butterfly: they say.
"The passing wind shakes the leaves
The bright moonlight pooled in the pond…"
The poem my mother used to recite, now has been folded
Like flower petals and flew into eternity with its master−
What should I do!
When I want to hear my mother's recitation again,
What should I really do?

[Note] Mother passed away peacefully, January 11, 2022 at 1pm.

아모르 파티

오면 반드시 가고
한 번 가면 다시 돌아오기 힘든 것
이는 자연의 법칙이며
진화와 멸종의 순리라 하네.
지극히 작고 유한한 생명체에 불과한 내가
전생에 무슨 좋은 업을 지었기에
이처럼 아름다운 창조주의 작품들을
무시로 누릴 자격이 주어졌는가?
공기, 빛, 물, 대지…
그리고 그대

어제의 숲을 지나와
오늘의 삶의 광장으로 흘러든 내가
무한한 내일들의 대양(大洋) 앞에서
인간으로, 단 하나뿐인 진정한 나의 나로
숨 쉬고 있음이여–
*아모르 파티!
경건하게, 아주 경건하게, 건배하고 싶네
그대에게, 나에게, 그리고 내 삶을 건드리고 간
기쁨과 슬픔 그리고 고통의 순간들에게.

Amor Fati

What comes, must go
Once it goes, it rarely returns
These are nature's law
The rule of evolution and extinction.
I am nothing but a microscopical mortal being,
And yet, what good deeds have I done
In my previous life to deserve
The almighty creator's beautiful works?
Air, light, water, earth⋯
And You!

Passed through the forest of yesterdays
Flowed into this living plaza of today
Standing before the infinite ocean of tomorrow
Breathing
As a human being; as one and only true me.
*Amor Fati!
Reverently, very reverently
I want to make a toast
To you, to me, and to every moment
Of the joy, sorrow and pain that touched my life.

✛ Book Review 1:

— Ariadne Sawyer

Poet Bong Ja Ahn's deeply moving new book 『Songs from the Lotusland』 is a brilliant and penetrating look at the life of an immigrant in Canada and her poetic life's work.

Her beautiful words portray clear images, include the reader as if they are traveling her journey with her. Such poems as 'The Fog' and 'Fragrance of Human Flower' show her poetic depth. 『Songs from the Lotusland』 is her 9th book and fourth volume of poetry in English. Also, the poems are carefully translated into Korean by herself.

I think that the author's literary work should be in university curriculum, providing others with insight and knowledge.

Ariadne Sawyer: MA, CC.; Author, Poet resides in Vancouver, Canada; Consultant; Founder of the World Poetry Reading Series Society, Host and producer of the World Poetry Cafe Radio Show and World Poetry Peace and Human Rights Festivals, Author of 4 books, 2017 Nobel Peace Prize Nominee.

✦ 서평 1:

— 아리아드니 소여

안봉자 시인의 감동적인 새 시집『로터스랜드에서 부르는 노래』는 캐나다 이민자의 삶과 그녀의 시적인 삶을 독자들에게 명확하고 깊숙이 보여준다.

그녀의 아름다운 시어들은 선명하게 이미지들을 묘사하며, 독자들로 하여금 그녀의 인생 여정을 함께 여행하는 것처럼 느끼게 한다. '안개'와 '인간 꽃향기' 같은 시들에서 우리는 그녀의 시적 깊이를 볼 수 있다.『로터스랜드에서 부르는 노래』는 안 시인의 아홉 권째 저서이자 네 권째 영/한 대역시집이며, 그녀의 시들은 모두 그녀가 직접 쓰고 번역했다.

나는 안 시인의 문학 작품은 대학교 커리큘럼에 넣어 다른 사람들에게 통찰력과 지식을 제공해야 한다고 생각한다.

아리아드니 소여: 작가, 맥클레인 헌터상 수상 시인, 캐나다 밴쿠버에 거주, 창작 예술 전문 상담가, 세계시낭송협회 창설자이며 초대 회장, 세계시낭송 카페 레디오 쇼 창시자/사회자, 2017년 노벨평화상 후보자.

✠ Book Review 2:

With longing and passion, Bong−Ja Ahn's poems offer adventurous threads along her traveled path.

Even during dark winters, her 9th book, 『Songs of the Lotusland』 encourages readers to treasure the beauty of the natural world. She writes: "⋯my dormant hopes revive every spring / and the spirit of poetry rises in me / on a pair of white wings."

With a gifted poet's eye, Bong−Ja grounds our hope in images of roses, tides, dandelions, and aurora night skies.

Betty Scott: An award−winning poet, writer, Educator and Editor resides in Bellingham, USA; Earned degrees from three universities, including U.C.L.A.; The author of "Central Heating: Poems that Celebrate Love, Loss and Planet Earth".

— 베티 스콧

안봉자의 시들은 그리움과 열정으로 그녀가 지나온 인생행로 위에 모험적인 실타래를 풀어서 우리에게 제공한다.

그녀의 아홉 번째 저서 『로터스랜드에서 부르는 노래』는 독자들에게 "…당신의 초록 둥지에서/잠자던 희망은 봄마다 다시 깨어나고/비상을 꿈꾸는 내 시혼(詩魂)의/하얀 날개 한 쌍/뜨겁게 날아오르기 때문입니다"라고 말하며, 춥고 어두운 겨울 속에서도 자연계의 아름다움을 소중히 여기도록 격려한다.

타고난 시적 재능의 눈을 가진 안봉자 시인은 장미, 조수(潮水), 민들레꽃, 밤하늘의 오로라 등의 이미지들에 우리의 희망을 심어준다.

베티 스콧: 수상 경력을 가진 시인, 작가, 미국 벨링햄 시(市)에 거주. 교육자 및 편집자. U.C.L.A. 센트럴 워싱턴 대학교와 웨스턴 워싱턴 대학교에서 학위 취득. 시집 『센트럴 난방 −사랑, 상실, 그리고 행성 지구를 경축하는 시』의 저자.

* Amor Fati: A Latin phrase for "love of fate", or "Love of one's fate": A positive attitude about life: the theory by the German philosopher Friedrich Nietzsche(1844–1900).

아모르 파티: 라틴어로 "네 운명을 사랑하라"는 뜻: 독일 철학자 프리드리히 니체(1844~1900)가 주장한 긍적적인 운명론.

* Applique Quilt: quilt that is made by using many pieces of different colour cloths stitched together.

조각보 이불: 여러 색깔의 천 조각들을 예쁘게 오려 붙여 만든 이불 커버.

* Barley Hump: refers to the period between May and June, when the fall harvest runs out but the barley is not yet ripe. Many Koreans in the past had to endure hunger during this period.

보릿고개: 5~6월, 식량 사정이 매우 어려운 시기를 의미하는 말로 춘궁기(春窮期)라고도 한다. 오래전 가난했던 한국의 봄철 기근을 말함.

* Cantabile: An Italian word, means 'singable' or 'songlike'.

칸타빌레: 이탈리안 음악 용어, 노래하듯이 부드럽게.

* Christ the Redeemer: the statue of the Christ(30m high and 635tons) located at the peak of the Corcovado Mountain, Rio de Janeiro, Brazil. One of the New Seven Wonders of the World.

구원의 예수상: 브라질 리우데자네이루의 코르코바도산 정상에 위치한 그리스도상(높이 30m, 무게 635t). 리우데자네이루와 브라질의 문화적 아이콘이며, 세계 7대 불가사의 중 하나임.

* Elbow touching: one of Greetings in the time of Covid–19, by extending elbow to touch instead of handshakes.

팔꿈치 건드리기: 코로나바이러스 유행병이 창궐할 때 사람들이 악

수 대신에 팔꿈치를 서로 건드려서 반가움을 표시하는 몸짓.

＊Fraser River: the longest river within British Columbia, Canada. Rises at Fraser Pass near Mount Robson in the Rocky Mountains and flows for 1,375km into the Strait of Georgia at the city of Vancouver. It is the 10th longest river in Canada.

프레이저강: 캐나다 브리티시 콜롬비아 주의 가장 긴 강. 로키 산맥 프레이저 재의 랍슨 산정 근처에 수원이 있으며, 밴쿠버 앞 조지아 해협으로 흘러들어 태평양과 만난다. 총 길이는 1375㎞, 캐나다에서 열 번째로 긴 강.

＊Form is Emptiness, Emptiness is Form: The main teaching of The Heart Sutra in Buddhism: everything in the world is constantly changing, so there is no reality, but everything is connected & all things exist in relationship.

색즉시공, 공즉시색(色卽是空, 空卽是色): 불교의 중심이 되는 경전인 반야심경(般若心經)의 핵심내용: 세상의 모든 것은 끊임없이 변하므로 실체가 없지만, 변하고 드러나지 않는 그 속에 모든 것은 서로 관계로 서 분명히 존재한다는 뜻.

＊Hansari: Spring−tide: Around the full moon and the last eve of the month on the lunar calendar, when the tide is at its highest.

한사리: 음력 보름과 그믐 무렵에 밀물이 가장 높은 때.

＊Imjingak Park: located on the banks of the Imjin River, 7km from the Military Demarcation Line in South Korea. There are many monuments regarding the Korean War.

임진각 공원: 한국의 군사 분계선에서 7㎞ 떨어진 임진강 유역에 위치하며, 한국 전쟁(1950~1953) 관련된 동상과 기념물이 많음.

＊Inuit: a group of culturally similar indigenous peoples, the majority of them inhabit the Arctic and subarctic regions of Greenland, Canada, and Alaska(USA).

이누이트: 알래스카주, 그린란드, 캐나다 북부와 시베리아 극동에 사는, 문화적으로 원주민들과 유사한 종족.

* Inter−being: a word that is not in the dictionary yet. It means the interconnectedness of everything that exists.

인터−빙: 상호 존재: 아직 한글 사전에 없는 단어로, 존재하는 모든 것의 상호 연결성을 의미함.

* Maple Leaf Country: Canada: The Canadian flag has one red maple leaf drawn in the middle. The maple leaf has been used as a Canadian emblem since the 18th century. The Canadian flag of today was adapted February 15, 1965.

단풍잎의 나라: 캐나다. 캐나다 국기는 복판에 빨간 단풍잎 한 개가 그려졌다. 단풍잎은 18세기부터 캐나다를 상징해왔으며, 오늘날 사용하는 캐나다 국기는 1965년 2월 15일에 채택되었다.

* Personal Legend: One's destiny in life. It's identifying your purpose in life and pursuing it. It has referred to in "The Alchemist" by the Brazilian Nobelist, Paulo Coelho.

자아의 신화: 삶의 목적을 갖고 추구하는 것이며, 이는 곧 자신의 꿈으로 통하는 오솔길이고 운명이다. 브라질 작가 '파울로 코엘료'의 소설 『연금술사』에서 언급되었음.

* Two hundred dollars: In 1970, the Republic of Korea government allowed immigrants abroad to take up to $200 only.

이민자의 유출 허용 금 2백 달러: 1970년, 가난했던 대한민국 정부는 해외 이민자들에게 200달러까지만 현금을 가지고 나가도록 허용했다.

* Winter Retreat: a three−month group meditation retreat in Buddhist Temple during winter season.

동안거: 불교 승려들이 겨울철 90일간 한 곳에 머물면서 수행 정진 하는 일.